HELD'S
ANGELS

JOHN HELD, JR. AND
FRANK B. GILBRETH, JR.

HELD'S ANGELS

NEW YORK

THOMAS Y. CROWELL COMPANY

HELD'S
ANGELS

CHAPTER 1

AT FORTY-SIX, Alfred J. College was no longer a handsome man, nor was he especially distinguished looking. Rather, he had the appearance of a Substantial Citizen, which he was, although not objectionably so.

Not bald, but balding. Not plump, but no longer lithesome. Not a reactionary, but admittedly tending toward conservatism.

A pleasant, upper-middle-class businessman — reliable, intelligent, and what is known as Reasonably Well Fixed. That was Alfred J.

An unworried man, you might think, if someone should point him out to you in the street. And you would be wrong. Because in recent months Alfred Joseph College had been toting on his sturdy shoulders a worry which, like the bottom half of an hourglass, grew heavier with the passing of every minute.

And time was running out.

The worry concerned his son, who was leaving home in a few days to enter Midwestern University. Richard was seventeen and generally considered by his contemporaries to be a perfectly normal male. He was black-haired, good-looking, and several inches taller than his father. He liked girls, owned a half interest in a hot-rod automobile, preferred sports shirts and sweaters to business suits, had outgrown his first tuxedo, had won his high-school letter in football, shaved every third day, had tried beer but didn't particularly like it, and smoked a package of cigarettes a week, mostly at social functions.

Alfred himself was a smoker and occasionally drank a highball. But he didn't approve of his son's becoming a slave either to nicotine or to alcohol. Alfred at one time had thought of offering

3

ONE MOTHER, ONE FATHER, ONE TONSIL-
EXPERT, FOUR GENERAL PRACTITIONERS,
THREE TRAINED NURSES, FIVE GOVERN-
ESSES, FIFTY-SIX ORDINARY TEACHERS,
THIRTY-TWO PROFESSORS, AND THREE
ATHLETIC TRAINERS COMBINED THEIR
EFFORTS TO PRODUCE THIS.

Richard a gold watch if he didn't smoke until he was twenty-one. But Richard already had a gold watch which he had bought with his own money, saved from summer jobs at a filling station. Mr. College also had had to stop the argument about growth-stunting, when Richard reached six feet and showed no inclination to level off.

Alfred never let up, though, on the evils of alcohol, the pitfalls of wild women, the hazards of hot-rods, and the permanently maiming possibilities of football. Particularly football of the variety played at Midwestern University.

Newspaper stories about the prevalence in certain cities of

marijuana smoking and non-virgin clubs among teen-agers were particularly upsetting to Alfred. He thanked the Good Lord that vice of that kind hadn't reached their city. Or had it? How was a father to know, when his son never took the time or trouble to confide in him?

Frankly, Mr. College was convinced that his son was much too immature and irresponsible to be cut loose from parental supervision. He didn't like the thought of Richard's being sent like a lamb to the wolves at Midwestern.

"The boy doesn't even dress like a man, let alone look, or think, or act like a man," Alfred complained to his wife, Betty. "Those God-awful sports shirts and yellow shoes! And every time he

FROM A FRESHMAN'S LETTER HOME
"DEAR MOTHER :—EVERY MORNING I EXERCISE WITH DUMBBELLS."

goes out with a girl in that hellish, souped-up, jet-propelled mowing machine of his, do you know what I have?"

"Indigestion?" Betty suggested.

"Nightmares. Sometimes he gets her in the family way, and sometimes he wraps both of them around a telephone pole. And if he thinks I'm going to stand one minute for his playing football at Midwestern, well, by George, he's got another think coming, and . . ."

"You don't know what the present generation's coming to, do you, Joe?" Betty interrupted gently.

"No, by God," said Alfred, raising his voice, "I don't. I do know it's a sin and a shame to let a youngster like that . . ." He broke off with a grin that was half sheepish and half nostalgic. It had been quite a few years since anyone had called him Joe.

It was the final quarter of the big game with Michigan. Joe guessed he never would forget that game if he lived to be fifty. He was a soph, and three days before he had been moved up from the scrubs to the varsity squad. You can't laugh that off!

He hadn't got in the Michigan game yet, and probably he wouldn't. But it was the first time he had sat on the bench, and even that was thrill enough for one day.

The speech that Coach Rusty Bent had given them at half-time was still ringing in his ears. Midwestern was trailing by seven to nothing at the half, but after old Rusty's fight talk the big team had caught fire and tied the score. Seven to seven, it stood now, in the dying minutes of the last quarter.

Joe hoped for old Rusty's sake, as well as for the sacred orange and black colors, that the big team would score again. It was going to be hard lines for old Rusty if the big team didn't win this one. Particularly since it was the coach's birthday, and all.

If the big team had only known at the start of the game that old Rusty's kid was practically on his deathbed, but still clutching

Him—But I say, what—
Her—It's quite all right, sir. I'm a daughter of the Abent-minded Professor, and I'm a bit absent-minded myself.

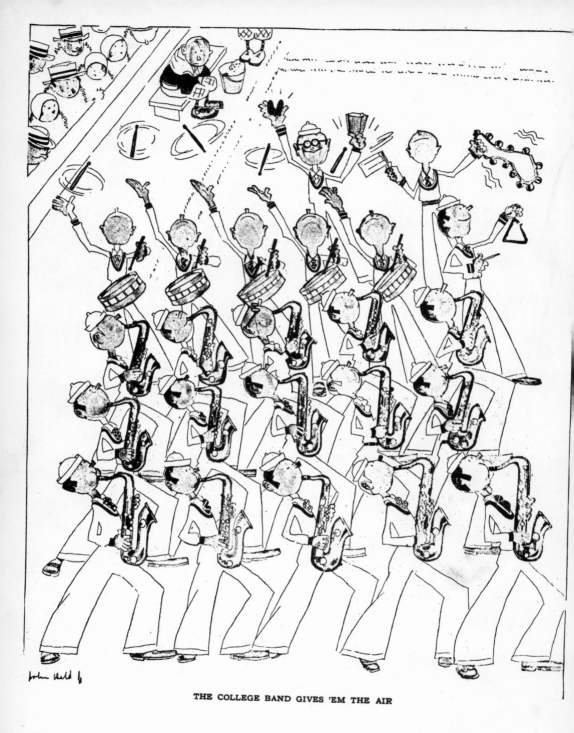

THE COLLEGE BAND GIVES 'EM THE AIR

the wireless headphones to get the latest scores — if the big team had known that they might have played as well during the first half as they had in the third quarter.

Joe wondered why Rusty hadn't told them earlier about that, and about his birthday, and about the fact that his contract hinged on victory, and about how he had personally promised President Carswell that his charges would bring back the traditional oaken bucket which belonged to the winner, and which now was held by Michigan.

Old Rusty was a close-mouthed clam, all right. If he hadn't got all excited there in the locker-room at half-time, he probably never would have let them know about all his troubles and responsibilities.

Joe fidgeted tensely as Midwestern took time out. An assistant manager raced out to the big team with a water bucket and dipper.

Joe wished that Rusty would put him in there, but he knew it wasn't likely. Since he weighed only 155 pounds, Joe had been forced to go out for quarterback. And the first-string quarterback was Fred Moulten, a senior All-American who had played the entire sixty minutes of every game so far this year.

The Midwestern cheerleaders, who had been doing acrobatics on the cinder track in front of the home stands, called for a locomotive. Megaphones went spinning into the air, and the sweater-clad cheerleaders crouched on one knee. Their fists went in tight circles, treadmill-wise.

"Sis," crashed the locomotive.

The thunder of the cheer rolled through the bowl.

"Boom."

Joe was surprised at how loud it sounded. He guessed it always sounded louder on the bench and on the field than it did in the stands.

"Ahhh. Midwestern! Team, team, teaaam!"

Up until today Joe had always been in the stands himself. He

The College Comics

knew how it was up there, wrapped in raccoon, hoarse from hollering, fortified with a snifter or two from a flask, friends with everyone. It was good; it was the cat's pajamas. Unless old Rusty were going to put him in there — and Joe told himself again there wasn't a chance of that — he almost wished he were up in there in the stands today.

Now time was back in again, and there wasn't much time left. Michigan's ball on its own thirty. Fourth down. The Wolverines went into kick formation and Fred Moulten back-pedaled into position to catch the punt. It was a high spiral, which Everready Freddie, as the newspapers called him, took nicely on the run. But two Michigan men tackled him hard around the ankles and he went down and stayed there.

THE GIRL WHO SAT ON THE WRONG SIDE OF THE FIELD

A groan rose from the Midwestern stands, and then an organized cheer. "Ray, Moulten. Ray, ray, Moulten."

Moulten wasn't going to play sixty minutes of this game. He managed to stand up, but his left foot stuck out sideways, instead of straight ahead, and it was obvious that his ankle was broken. Rusty gave a signal from the bench and four men carried Moulten to the sidelines. He was crying, and he kept repeating: "Old Rusty didn't have to take me out. I ain't no teahound!"

Rusty walked up and down in front of the bench, and Joe's

hands started to sweat. He dropped his army blanket, so that Rusty would be sure to see him. He was scared, but he knew that if they put him in there he'd get a touchdown somehow.

Rusty didn't even look his way.

"Whipple," said Rusty, and another substitute quarterback jumped to his feet, grabbed a helmet, did a couple of deep-knee bends, and ran eagerly to the coach.

Rusty and Whipple held a whispered conference, and then the coach slapped him on the rear and sent him into the game. Joe's hands stopped sweating, and he pulled the army blanket up over his head again. But he couldn't help hoping that what happened to Everready Freddie would happen to Whipple, only quicker and more so.

Midwestern's ball on its thirty-two. Two minutes to play. Whipple seemed nervous. He was dancing around behind the center, and his voice sounded shrill as he called the signals. The center passed him the ball, and Whipple dropped it. He managed to recover the ball, but the play lost three yards. Rusty buried his face in his hands.

The big team lined up again. Whipple seemed more nervous than ever. Again the ball was passed to him, and again he dropped it and recovered. Rusty was on his feet now, his hands raised to Heaven, and cursing at the top of his voice.

Joe was on his feet, too. He couldn't help it. He ran to Rusty, grabbed him by the shoulders, and shook him.

"Put me in, Coach," he begged. "Put me in."

"Who in the hell are you, anyway?" screamed Rusty, as if this were the final indignation to heap upon a man whom the gods already had ground exceeding small.

"Joe College, sir. I know I can get a touchdown if you'll give me a chance. I keep thinking about the old oaken bucket, and that boy of yours with the headphones, and . . . I know I can do it, Coach!"

"Oh, yeah?" Rusty bellowed sarcastically.

Hold 'em

The Freshman Who Cut in
on the Football Captain

"Yeah," Joe replied firmly.

Rusty looked at him intently, and then handed him a helmet.

"By golly," said the coach, "I believe you can. All right, boy, get in there. And fight!"

Joe went in there. He remembered to report to the referee, and then took Whipple's place behind the center. Fifty-five seconds to go. Midwestern's ball on its own twenty-five. Third down.

"Never mind the signals," Joe ordered. "Just give me the ball when I say 'hike.' Ready, hike."

The center gave him the pigskin, and he tucked it under his left arm and started around right end. Joe was fast, which was why he had been moved up to the varsity squad despite his lack of weight. He danced around a big Michigan tackle who had come charging through the line, and he stiff-armed a Michigan end. Then he was in the clear and running. He sidestepped a half-back as he crossed the midfield stripe, but before he could get back into his stride the Michigan quarterback was on him and cut him down. As he fell, he tucked the ball into his stomach and hugged it with both arms. No matter what happened, he wasn't going to drop it.

He felt some other players land on him, and he felt his left kneecap give way in a searing flash of pain. But even before the pile had untangled he had raised his head and one arm to shout for time out, so as to stop the clock.

Everyone in the bowl was on his feet now, and Joe heard a tremendous cheer go up from the Midwestern stands. "Ray, thirty-two. Ray, ray, thirty-two." Thirty-two was Joe's number. Apparently the cheerleaders didn't know his name and didn't have time to find out.

He was careful not to limp, when they lined up again. He didn't want Rusty to know about that knee. Five seconds to go. The pain was sickening. Midwestern's ball on the Wolverines' 25.

"When I say 'hike,' just give me the ball," he barked, while they waited for time to be called in again. He didn't know he was

He Told Her He'd

ing a Coonskin Coat.

sobbing. He jerked off his helmet and threw it to the sidelines. The Midwestern stands went wild.

The referee signaled, and Joe hollered "hike." Michigan was looking for him to try the ends again, or to throw a last desperate pass. A 155-pound quarterback couldn't be expected to crack the line.

But Joe saw a six-inch hole and hipped his way through it, before it could close. His momentum carried him into the Michigan secondary. And on he streaked — a thin, black-haired kid running with a limp. But how he was running!

He made a full pivot, and a Michigan halfback who had dived at him got nothing but an armful of frozen sod. Joe regained his stride in time to pivot again and lose the other halfback. But each pivot had cost him time, and three Michigan linesmen who were trailing him were closing the gap.

And still he kept running, until he was within five yards of the goal posts, in whose shadow the Wolverine safety man was crouched and balanced to bring him down. There was no time to dodge, because the men at his heels were poised to strike.

Joe shoved the pigskin into his stomach and dove. As he did so, the three men behind him and the one man in front of him also dove.

That was all he remembered. He was unconscious on the sidelines, in Rusty Bent's arms, when Midwestern dropkicked the extra point for a fourteen to seven victory and possession of the oaken bucket.

When Joe finally came to, he was in the big team's private locker room, lying on a rubbing table. Someone had taken off his uniform, and he could still smell spirits of ammonia in his nostrils. His knee hurt and his head was throbbing.

"Busted kneecap and concussion," Doc Barker was saying. "He'll be all right. But he'll never play football again — not with that knee. It's going to give him trouble for the rest of his life."

He saw old Rusty standing nearby, and a group of men he

She "Made" the Team

guessed were sports writers. Old Rusty was the one who was
crying now.

"Did we win it, Rusty?" he managed to whisper.

"We won it, boy."

"Did I make the touchdown?"

"You made it, boy," choked Rusty, sponging his tears with a
soggy bath towel. "You made it with a broken kneecap and with
half the Michigan team riding on your back. You're the campus
hero."

"What did you say his name was?" one of the reporters interrupted impatiently. "His number's thirty-two, but it isn't even on
the roster and your spotters in the press box couldn't identify
him."

"He's new on the varsity squad this week," Rusty explained.

"You fellows get out of here and let him rest," Doc Barker
demanded. "He's a mighty sick boy."

"But what's his name?" the reporter insisted.

Joe felt himself slipping back to unconsciousness, but Rusty came over and patted him gently on the shoulder, and he pulled himself out of it.

"What did you say your name was, boy?" Rusty asked.

"Joe College, Coach," said Joe.

CHAPTER 2

"I DON'T MEAN," Alfred J. was telling his wife, "that Richard is any worse than other boys his age. Although God knows that's not saying much. What he really lacks is a sense of responsibility."

"I guess all boys lack that," said Betty.

"And those stories you read about kids smoking marijuana. Maybe it's only newspaper talk, but when we were kids we wouldn't even have thought of such a thing."

"Especially," she nodded, "since we never *did* think of it."

"Liquor's what I worry most about though."

"But he doesn't drink, you know that."

"Not now, no," Alfred said darkly. "Not while we're around to keep an eye on him. But what's going to happen when he's on his own? He might get too much to drink, make a complete fool of himself, and even . . ."

"Get himself arrested and disgrace us all?" Betty asked innocently.

Joe was sitting in a leather armchair, between the "No Parking Here" and "Reserved for Police" signs in the oak-paneled reception room of his fraternity house. It had been almost two weeks since he had won the Michigan game, and except for the cast on his knee it all seemed like a pleasant dream.

The doctors said his knee was healing nicely. Joe put a good deal more faith in the doctors than he did in the Coué theory, but he thought it best not to overlook any bets. Consequently, whenever he thought of the theory, he played things safe by repeating that every day in every way the knee was getting better and better.

Joe had managed to catch up with his studies, after being released from the university hospital, and now was catching up on the last issue of *College Humor*. It was Thursday night, and he had already done his homework for Friday.

Joe and a freshie who was on late duty to run errands had the whole downstairs to themselves. Everyone else was upstairs studying. Joe guessed a lot of people who thought college boys were a bunch of stews would be surprised at how much real studying went on during the week.

"Here's a hot one," Joe told the pledge. "He says, 'Why are you wearing two sets of garters?' And she says, 'One pair to hold up stockings and the other to hold up traffic.'"

The freshman, who had already read the magazine but was flattered by this attention from a sophomore and campus hero, went into dutiful spasms of laughter. "That's a hot one, I don't mean maybe," he gasped.

"How about this?" Joe continued. "She says, 'Is my nose shiny, sweetie?' And he says, 'No, but your right knee is dusty.'"

The pledge roared again, this time perhaps overdoing it by falling out of his chair and writhing in mirth on the rug.

"For John's sake, don't knock yourself out," Joe warned.

"I don't mean maybe," repeated the freshman, still laughing dutifully.

The doorbell rang, and the freshie picked himself up from the floor.

"Wonder who that is?" he asked.

"I'll bite," said Joe. "You'd better go see."

The freshman went to the door. All pledges had been carefully schooled in how to greet various callers. At first Joe couldn't hear exactly what the freshman was saying, but the warm tone of hospitality in his voice indicated that the visitor was a college official, a parent of one of the brothers, the traveling secretary of the national fraternity who sometimes dropped in unexpectedly on inspection trips, or a bootlegger.

"Fan my brow, if it's not good to see you, Mickey," Joe heard the pledge declare as he led the visitor through the front hall. "Press the flesh, boy, press the flesh. It's a real pleasure, I'll tell the cockeyed world."

Mickey came in, a middle-aged man dressed like a college boy in Oxford bags, porkpie hat and a bearskin coat which swept the floor. Mickey always looked fat when he entered the house, but, after he produced a dozen or so bottles from various nooks and crannies under the coat, his weight came down to normal.

"Hi, Mick," Joe hollered cordially. "What kind of poison are you selling tonight?"

"I don't like no talk about poison," pouted Mickey, whose moods were unpredictable and who sometimes didn't like to be kidded. "I went to a lot of trouble to get this pre-war stuff for you boys."

"I was only spoofing," Joe hastened to assure him.

"I don't like no spoofing about poison. Go ahead and drain the stuff off the corpses in the medical lab, if you'd rather have that than pre-war stuff."

"We like your stuff fine," Joe apologized. He thought it best not to add that the medical college, noting a disappearance that even the most broad-minded of professors could no longer attribute to evaporation, now kept its alcohol in a vault.

Somewhat mollified, Mickey continued to unload himself. Both he and Joe knew that the social standing of a fraternity could be

The Pilgrim Fathers Gave Thanks for Dry Land

THANKSGIVING

by John Held, Jr.

And Now We Have the Dry Land!

THE LASS WHO LOVED A SAILOR

judged fairly accurately by the number and caliber of its boot-leggers. A fraternity without *any* bootleggers was considered to be in as bad shape as a fraternity without pledges.

The freshman departed to relay the glad tidings of Mickey's arrival, and Joe limped over to the table where the bootlegger was placing the bottles.

"Pre-war Golden Wedding," said Mickey, as Joe picked up a bottle and examined it.

"Is that Scotch or rye?" asked Joe, really seeking information.

"Golden Wedding," said Mickey, "is, er . . ." He picked up a bottle himself and read the label. "Golden Wedding is rye whiskey."

"Oh," said Joe, admiring the label and the official-looking stamps over the cork. He turned the bottle upside down to see if the bottom had been scissored, but he couldn't see any signs that it had been. He noticed that some black specks of charcoal were floating in the pale yellow fluid. Joe knew that was a sign it had been aged.

"Mind if I test it, Mickey?" he asked. "I guess it's pre-war, all right. But there's one test that never fails — the blue flame test."

"Sure," said Mickey, who had regained some of his good humor, "go ahead and test it. I'd do the same myself. You can't be too careful about what you drink."

With studied nonchalance, Joe took a folding corkscrew from one end of his watch chain.

"I always carry one of these," he said proudly.

Then he opened the bottle and poured about a thimble of the liquor into an ashtray. The fraternity brothers began arriving in the reception room, and they gathered around as Joe lit a match and touched it to the ashtray. The liquor caught fire.

"It's good stuff, all right," Joe conceded. "That flame is really *blue!*"

"I never seen a bluer," Mickey conceded smugly. "Like I told you, it's pre-war."

The fumes from the open bottle were not pleasant. Joe re-corked it, and bought the quart. With a football weekend coming up, Mickey's original load was soon purchased, but he had more outside in his Pierce Arrow roadster. He left the house a man of average weight, and returned in a few moments as a fat man. He made two other trips before all of his customers were satisfied.

On a football weekend, the old grads started arriving at the fraternity house late Friday afternoon. Some of them were pretty stewed when they got there, and all of them were pretty stewed by supper time. So were some of the actives. A few of the old grads were stinko, a condition also known as being stewed to the eyebrows.

The house served a buffet supper Friday night, but most of the group never got around to eating.

The alumni brought their hooch with them, in silver hip flasks and with a spare quart or two of emergency rations in their suitcases.

For the first hour or so, the alumni and the actives didn't get along any too congenially. The alumni thought the actives were too young to make fools of themselves by drinking, and the actives thought the alumni were too old to make fools of them-selves by drinking. The uncongeniality wore off as the evening progressed, and disappeared completely by the time of the bonfire and pep rally later that night.

In general, strict rules of etiquette were attached to the process of taking a drink in the house on Friday evenings. The etiquette amounted to shrouding the drink-taking in a cloak of secrecy which was purposely made so dramatic that everyone knew the secret.

The drinkers, who constituted a unanimous majority, wanted to be sure that everyone knew they were drinking. At the same time, they wanted to be sure that everyone also knew they weren't advertising the fact that they were drinking.

Admittedly, this was fairly involved. What it boiled down to

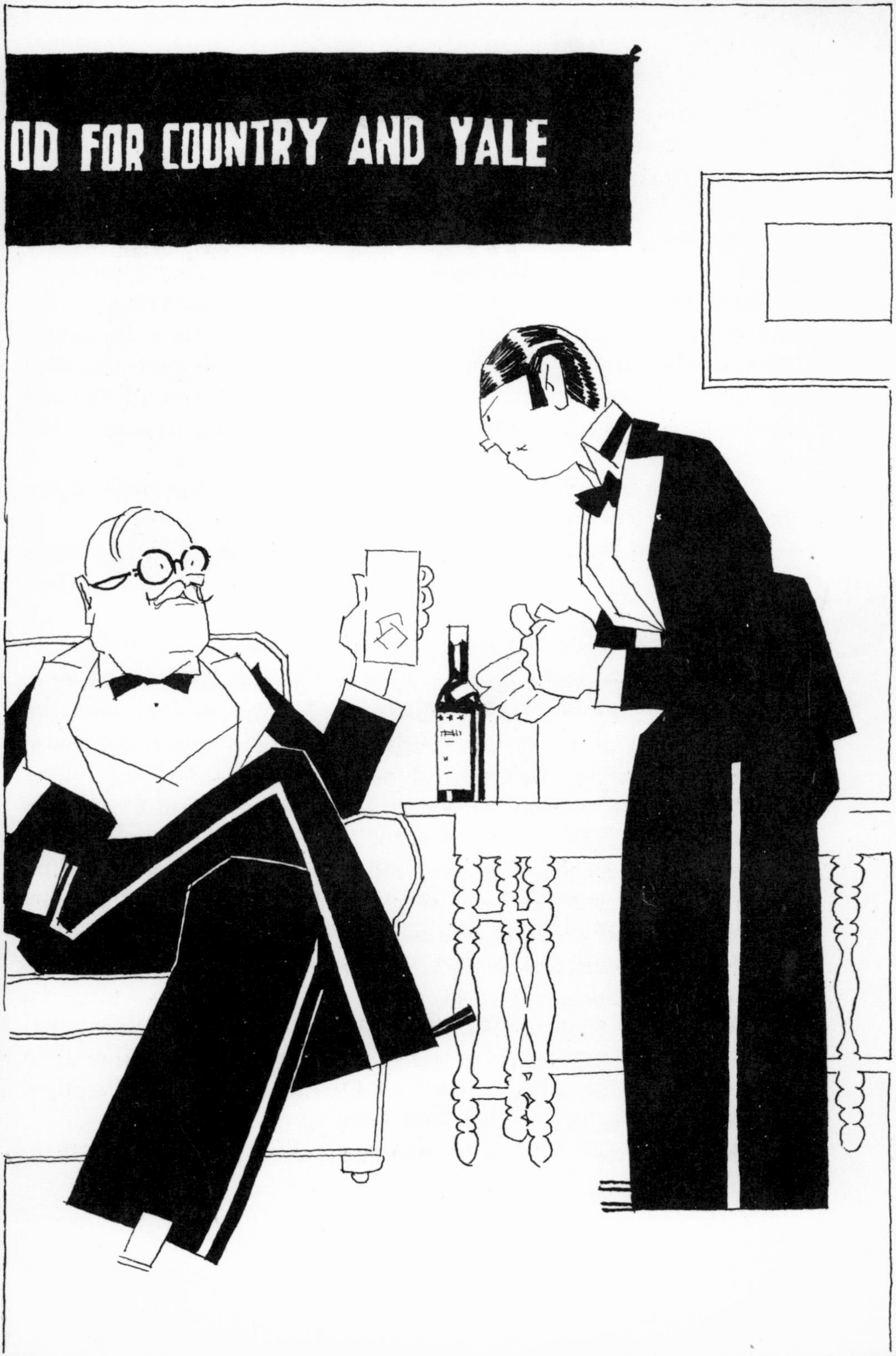
OD FOR COUNTRY AND YALE

"This liquor tastes like insecticide."
"Yes—it isn't Flit to drink."

was this: Unless you were some kind of a blue-nosed Prohibitionist or other species of killjoy, you drank. But if you ostentatiously paraded your drinking, you were considered a smart aleck and, even worse, acting like a rah-rah boy.

Obviously, a person didn't wish to be considered a Prohibitionist or killjoy, so he wanted everyone to know he was drinking. Obviously, a person didn't wish to be considered a smart aleck or rah-rah boy, so he hid his drinking with secrecy as dramatic and unsecret as a coloratura's stage whisper.

Thus one alumnus would get out of his chair and walk conspirator-fashion around the room, nudging and also whispering in the ears of four or five other alumni and perhaps an active member or two. Then they and their wives or dates would arise, nudge each other some more, and file out of the living room to the back hall or one of the bedrooms.

The etiquette, on the part of those remaining in the living

room, called for aiding and abetting the act of making the secret
an open one.

"Hey, where you stiffs going?" someone would call to the
departing group.

"To see a man about a dog," was the generally accepted re-
joinder. This was accompanied by winks and still more nudges.

If the party were fairly well under way, someone might also go
so far as to speculate on the possibility that a member of the
canine family had actually manufactured whatever it was that
those departing were going to see about.

It was a game which had the merit of including everyone in a
delightful charade of derring-do, a game in which all the participants shared a secret and thus were brought, at least for a time,
into a bond of friendship which transcended the barriers of age
and sex and short acquaintance.

A GOOD ALL AROUND MAN

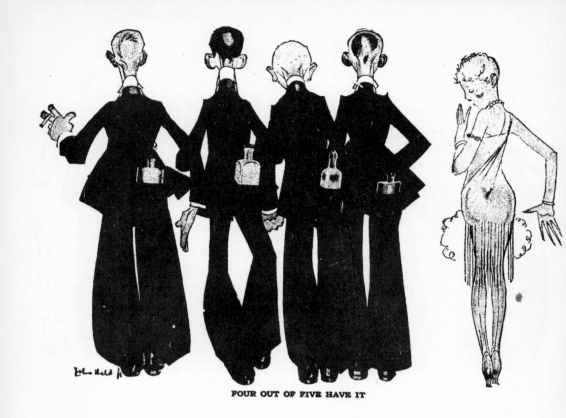

FOUR OUT OF FIVE HAVE IT

It was a game which, in later years, would leave some of its original participants with a subconscious void that could never be filled. Getting stewed would not fill it, because it was the game, not the getting stewed, which contained the derring-do. Revisiting college for a football weekend would not fill it, again because it was the game of the conspirators, not the football game, which was touched with the nostalgic magic. And when the game of Prohibition drinking was dead, it could not be revived simply by returning to the original scene, going through the motions of getting plastered, and making a general ass of oneself in the immediate vicinity of a new generation which could never understand the game. The game was dead, and so was youth. And college, if Joe and his friends had but known it, was youth's last stand.

BURNING THE MIDNIGHT OIL

Once the conspirators, who had left to see about the dog, reached the privacy of the hall or a bedroom, the flasks appeared and a comparison of the various contents ensued. The flasks were passed around for everyone to smell. Some of the connoisseurs poured a few drops on their palms and rubbed them briskly together, while sniffing with palpitating nostrils and ecstatic smiles the stomach-turning fumes.

"Smooth," they said, blinking back the tears.

"Downright smooth, I calls it."

They then described when and how they had got their liquor, and how much it had cost. The rye was positively guaranteed to be pre-war stuff, and the Scotch invariably was right off the boat.

Many of the flasks contained straight liquor and others contained private concoctions designed with an eye to the individual's taste for downright smoothness. Some of the whiskey — any liquor which wasn't colorless was whiskey — was diluted with prune juice, which everyone knew would counteract the fusel oil and minimize the effects of the ether. Some of the gin was diluted with orange juice. Straight alkie usually was diluted with canned grapefruit juice.

The act of taking a drink was postponed, perhaps unconsciously, for as long as decently possible. Like contemplating a dive into an icy lake, the thought of actually swallowing the downright smooth stuff was apt to provoke shivers along the spinal column. No one wanted to go first, but all knew that the way eventually to do it was to take it in one plunge — and that afterward it would feel wonderful.

"Well," some intrepid member of the group would declare at last, "here's how."

"Down the hatch," his companions would encourage him.

He'd show them how, tilting the flask, screwing up his face, swallowing four or five times, untilting the flask, shuddering, gulping, gagging and finally managing to suck in a deep breath of cooling air.

"Smooth," he'd crow, proud of his courage and not envying the chore still confronting his companions.

As Friday evening progressed, the etiquette about leaving the central rooms before taking a drink began to be ignored by the old grads. Most of the flasks were empty and the emergency rations were produced openly and put on the floor and tables. Gingerale, oranges, sugar, and ice were brought in from the kitchen. But Friday night wasn't the real night for drinking — for bottoms-up drinking. Bottoms-up drinking came on Saturday night, after the game. Friday was the night of the bonfire and pep rally.

Sunny Nash, Midwestern's immortal fullback of 1908–11, who had personally tallied 37 points in one game against Harvard and who never had missed a dropkick from within the thirty-five-yard

A IS FOR ANXIOUS, THATS HOW THEY ACT

EXTRACTS

from the

ALPHABET

of the

YOUNGER

or more

RISING GENERATION

by
John Held, Jr.

B IS FOR BOILED ON LEMON EXTRACT

(Continued next week)

line, was speaking at the pep rally. Joe may have felt just the
least bit wozzy at the pep rally, but at least he knew where he
was, which was more than some of the old grads who were
present would be able truthfully to say.

The fact was that Joe had been on his best behavior throughout
the fall term of his sophomore year. There had been a few unfortunate incidents during his freshman year of which his father had
particularly disapproved. The old man, of course, didn't understand the younger generation, but he did understand about Joe's
allowance, and he had threatened to cut it off.

So Joe was able to pay fairly close attention when Sunny, who
was now bald and fat, informed the student body that if they
showed the right kind of school spirit tomorrow, the big team
couldn't lose.

They gave three rahs and a bulldog for Sunny, and one of the
cheerleaders noticed Joe and they gave three rahs and a bulldog
for him, too. Joe sure thought it was swell to be the campus hero.

Midwestern's mascot, an aged ram named Billy, was paraded
across the platform, and the band played the alma mater, "Hail,
All Hail to Thee," while the men uncovered, and fat Sunny started
to blubber.

Finally, the bonfire was lit. The wood had been collected
during the week by freshmen, and as usual a small building from
a farmer's backyard was at the apex of the pile.

Pep rallies were the nuts, Joe thought, but after all they were
only a preliminary to the real thing. The real thing was on
Saturday.

Joe had a slight hangover Saturday morning, but nothing that
tomato juice wouldn't fix. He wished he had remembered, though,
to swallow olive oil before he started drinking Friday. Olive oil
was supposed to line your stomach and not only help you hold
more booze, but to preclude a hangover. He always meant to try it.

EXTRACTS

from the

ALPHABET

of the

YOUNGER

or more

RISING
GENERATION

C IS FOR CRISCO TO PUT ON THE HAIR

by
JOHN HELD, JR.

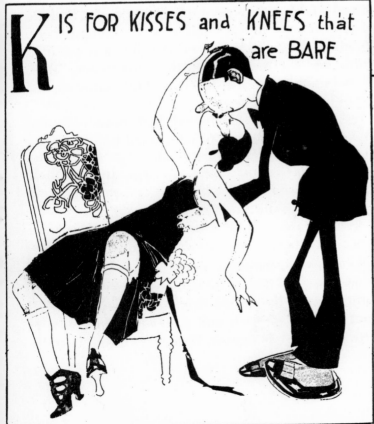

K IS FOR KISSES and KNEES that are BARE

The house served late breakfast on football Saturdays, and the previous uncongeniality between the actives and the old grads had somehow returned.

The old grads proudly compared hangovers and whispered about how the actives were too young to drink, couldn't tell the difference between rotgut and the real stuff, and might blind themselves or end up in the morgue. In order to regain some of their dignity, the alumni talked authoritatively about Mr. Coolidge, business, and the stock market. They passed along, in the strictest confidence, inside tips about stocks on which the wise boys — including themselves, naturally — intended to make a killing. They agreed that anyone who didn't get into the market on margin was a sucker. Nothing else but!

For their part, the actives whispered that a butter-and-egg man should be old enough either to hold his hooch or leave it alone. The consensus was that the old grads were dumbbells who had better wise up.

In both camps, particularly the butter-and-egg camp, there was considerable good-humored speculation about the medicinal effect of dosing oneself with the hair of the dog.

More and more old grads arrived during the morning, and most of them sought out Joe, thumped him on the back for beating Michigan, and offered him an eye-opener.

But Joe wasn't having any — at least not until the game. He was going to the game with his freshman baby, and she always got all hot and bothered if he showed up with the start of a skinful. She'd take a few drinks herself, but she didn't believe in skinfuls.

Joe took considerable care with his dress, because his freshman mama really was a snaky flapper, and he wanted to be at his best.

He had shaved and showered before breakfast and now, in his BVDs, he started work on his hair. His hair had a slight tendency to curl, so it required more attention than otherwise. First, he wet his hair by putting his head in a washbasin, dried it slightly, and added a gooey palmful of a pink substance known as Stacomb.

Extracts
from the
Alphabet
*of the Younger
or more Rising
Generation*

G IS FOR GIN
THAT WILL EAT
HOLES IN ZINC

S IS SLOW-MOTION,
NOTHING TO DRINK

by

John Held, Jr.

the mule-taming, dog-raising, rough-riding philosopher of Westport, Conn.

He rubbed this in well, and combed his locks down over his face. The front strands reached almost to his chin. Then he parted it in the middle and slicked it almost straight back. It clung in place with a patent-leather sheen, as if it were glued to his scalp, which it virtually was.

After cleaning the grease off his hands, he slipped into knee-length woolen socks with red, yellow and green diamonds on them; black shoes; plus-eight, checked knickers which bagged down almost to his shoes, thus mercifully hiding most of the socks; a white shirt; a jazzbow tie, this being a bow on an elastic; and a four-button single-breasted coat.

He looked in the mirror and was rather pleased with himself.

"WHY SO PENSIVE, SPIKE?"
"I WAS THINKING OF A FUNNY COSTUME TO WEAR AT THE MASKED BALL."

The raccoon calls on his mate.

Not a sheik, maybe, but certainly he'd pass in a crowd if you gave him a shove.

A flask filled with Mickey's Golden Wedding went into the breast pocket of the sackcoat. The weather was threatening and not cold enough for his raccoon, so he donned his yellow slicker. This was adorned with an oil painting of a flapper, oil paintings of various college pennants, and assorted messages in ink. The messages included "Why Girls Leave Home," "Bottoms Up," "I'll Move Over, Mama—There's Room for Two Inside," and "Chicken, Here's Your Roost."

Joe then put on his porkpie, which was shaped like the surface of a tailor's goose, with the point at the front, and which he wore on the back of his head. Last of all, he placed between his teeth a straight-stem pipe whose bowl sported a silver "M."

Midwestern won that game, too, defeating Wisconsin handily. Joe's date was named Elizabeth Coed and she was known as Betty. She had brought along two Midwestern pennants for them to wave, and two straws so that they could take a snort or two from Joe's flask without having to remove it from his pocket.

"A gal's got to be careful of her rep," she explained to Joe when she produced the straws. "I don't want people to get the idea that I'm fast."

"Does your mother know you're out?" Joe teased.

"Oh, horsefeathers!" smiled Betty.

She didn't drink much, and neither did Joe. And there really wasn't much sense in her worrying about her rep, because flasks were in evidence on all sides. Every time Midwestern scored, people would throw their arms around each other, bat each other over the head with programs, and scream hoarsely. During the second half, a few of the more unsteady imbibers went peacefully to sleep.

When the game was over, Betty and Joe stayed in the stands to watch the snake-dance, which wound around the goal posts and which finally snaked across the campus and into town. They would have taken part in the dance themselves, except for Joe's knee. Holding to Betty's arm, he managed to walk without too much trouble back to the fraternity house. Betty wasn't a very reliable support herself, because her open galoshes occasionally got caught together.

At the fraternity house, a wassail bowl was making the rounds to the accompaniment of noisy song. As Joe and Betty entered, the bowl was thrust into Joe's hands, and the crowded room took up the refrain:

> Here's to Brother College, tried and true;
> He's a drunkard through and through.
> He won't let us dance and he won't let us sing
> He won't let us do a goddamned thing.
> So drink, Brother College, Drink, Brother College
> . . . .
> Drinnnnnnnk.

Joe drank. You were supposed to keep drinking all through the last note of the song, which was extended as long as the breath of the singers held out. Joe was glad he had gone easy on Mickey's rye.

Betty passed up the wassail bowl, and so did Joe after the first round. But most of the butter-and-egg men continued to take their turns. Some of them, after five or six turns, would suddenly become green and make a hasty if staggering exit. They'd reappear a few minutes later, pale but game, and ready to accept the bowl again.

As someone has remarked, the acid test of a gentleman during Prohibition was whether he could throw up without getting anything on his shoes.

Joe was a little worried because the Feds — Prohibition agents — occasionally raided fraternity houses on football Saturdays, and the party seemed to be getting out of hand. If there were going to be any raids this Saturday, Joe figured his house was certainly asking for trouble.

Betty had the same thought, so they decided to get out of there. They put on their slickers and headed for The Green Parrot, a soda and sandwich shop across the street from the campus. The Green Parrot wasn't a blind pig, but the management didn't object if patrons spiked their Cokes — providing flasks and bottles were kept out of sight.

Joe ordered Cokes and was spiking them under the table when the Feds and local police raided The Green Parrot for the first time in its history. As the officers came in the front and back doors, the drinkers pushed out three windows and departed.

All of the drinkers, that is, except Joe, whose knee hurt too much to go through a window, and Betty, who may have decided to stick with Joe or who may have been prevented from moving when her galoshes got stuck together.

At any rate, Joe had no time either to empty or hide his flask, before one of the local policemen swooped down on him and grabbed it out of his hand.

"Gin," crowed the local officer, while some of the Feds gathered around to smell.

"Rye," corrected Joe miserably. He wondered what his father was going to say.

"Ain't I," asked the local officer, squinting into Joe's face, "seen you somewhere before?"

"His picture was in all the papers two weeks ago, when he won the Michigan game," Betty said defensively.

"I don't mean his pitcher. I mean *him*. Ain't I?" He poked a finger accusingly into Joe's face.

"I hope not, sir," said Joe.

The officer withdrew his finger and snapped it.

"I don't never forget a face," he said. "Last year. You was the one we caught after you tied a pair of pink bloomers to the top of the flagpole over the City Hall."

"My cow," Betty groaned. "Did you do that, too, Joe?"

"Me?" Joe was the picture of injured innocence.

"Joe College," shouted the officer, snapping his fingers again. "He's the one, all right. It took three days, and we finally had to get a steeplejack from Chicago, before we could get them damn bloomers down."

"Come clean, Joe," advised one of the Feds. "There's such a thing as fingerprints, you know. We'll find out if you have a record."

"But, good night, the bloomers were part of initiation," Joe protested. "If you bring them up again, my old man . . ."

"We ain't holding you for bloomers. This time we're holding you for booze," said the local officer.

The next day, the morning papers announced in black type: "Feds Raid Campus Hangout." In slightly smaller type, but still easily readable from a distance of a country mile was a sub-head, adding: "Flask-toting Joe College Forfeits Bond. Betty Coed Freed."

THE HIGHER EDUCATION
Relative to Practical Economics

For example—the black slicker of the frosh

—which is replaced with a yellow slicker at the passing of the first collegiate year—

Then to the male parent falls the lot of the black slicker—thus the equalization!

CHAPTER 3

"THE TROUBLE WITH HIGH SCHOOLS TODAY," pronounced Alfred College, "is that they don't teach children how to *study*. Richard hasn't the slightest idea of how to concentrate."

"He studies every school night," Betty pointed out, "and his grades were better than average."

"After seeing some of the mental cases of both sexes that Richard runs around with, I can understand why the average is low."

"But you've seen him yourself, down here every night studying, except on week ends," said Betty.

"I don't call it studying," grunted Alfred, "simply because a person holds a textbook in his hand. Especially when the person is sweating out a baseball game on television, sweating out the top tunes of the *Hit Parade* from a blaring radio in the next room, swilling root beer or some other unspeakable bellywash, and keeping tabs via telephone on the whereabouts of some twenty or thirty roving teen-agers. Richard's got to learn someday how to put his whole mind on what he's doing — or, believe me, he won't last one semester at Midwestern."

Joe shared a room at the fraternity house with two other sophs. They were both fine fellows. Joe thought they were swell eggs.

None of the three took college too seriously, but all of them realized the importance of passing their studies. Students who failed were kicked out of college, and that meant getting a job and going to work. The very thought of such an unpleasant prospect was enough to cause Joe, Fred, and Doc to buckle down to cramming sessions at which you could almost hear a pin drop, especially if it were of the bowling variety of pin.

COMPARATIVE ANATOMY

SOCIOLOGY

CHEMISTRY

Returns ~ by John Held Jr.

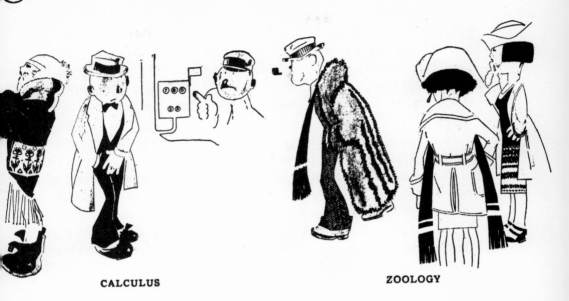

CALCULUS   ZOOLOGY

ENTOMOLOGY   MUSIC

The three did about the same amount of studying, but there was a wide difference in their grades. Fred Carter, who played the saxophone and was almost exactly Joe's size, had a photographic mind and seemed to be headed for Phi Beta Kappa. Joe, who played the traps, was a little better than average student. Doc Weaver, a good-natured fat boy who played the banjo and mandolin, barely limped through with passing grades and thus lived under a very real shadow of becoming his own breadwinner.

Not that it had anything to do with their scholastic attainments, but all three boys also played the ukulele.

Doc was somewhat of an idle dreamer. He dreamed about girls, but was painfully bashful in their presence and seldom went out with them. Still he talked about them almost constantly.

Doc's favorite pastime, and in fact a pastime which got a good deal more attention than it deserved from the entire fraternity, was speculation about the amount of underwear worn by various coeds.

While certainly not speaking from data collected through personal exploration, Doc nevertheless professed positive knowledge concerning the bloomers or teddies or lack of same of every coed in the classes he attended.

Perhaps it was a coincidence, but fate seemed to have assigned to Doc's classes an almost unanimous majority of females who didn't wear a blessed stitch under their dresses. The coincidence was the more remarkable, if true, in that it had occurred for two years running — in Doc's freshman as well as his sophomore years.

Doc made no claim to the possession of X-ray eyes. It was simply that he, more than any other member of the fraternity, apparently had the good fortune of being thrown into daily contact with various mamas who crossed their knees with reckless, uninhibited abandon; who revealed, to an admittedly appreciative if one-man audience, not only their rolled stockings and bare knees, but several acres of thigh and sometimes even more than

It Won't Be Long Now.

that; and who, in fact, seemed delightfully intent on subjecting themselves to prosecution for indecent exposure.

Doc liked nothing better than to take his entranced fraternity brothers on vicarious sightseeing tours of classroom after classroom peopled by shapely females whose crossings and uncrossings defied the laws of perpetual motion.

"And I'll swear — no kidding — I saw all the way up to *here*," Doc would wheeze and gesture from an armchair as he pointed solemnly to a spot about an inch above his navel while he crossed and uncrossed his own fat legs, making them go in sweeping, revealing circles which carried his feet up higher than his head.

Doc had one other, and much more serious, vice: he wanted to learn to tap dance, so that he could try out for the annual all-male Sword and Blade show — a sort of campus musical comedy. Doc had no natural talent along this line, but he practiced faithfully. Because of his weight, his practicing made the furniture rattle, and the fraternity house committee had been forced to rule that he could tap only in his own room. This made him somewhat less than an ideal roommate, but both Fred and Joe agreed that Doc had good traits which more than balanced this bad one.

None of the roommates was very tidy, except in dress, and their room in the fraternity house invariably was a shambles. If it takes a heap o' living in a house to make it home, they at least did their part by providing the heap.

Dresser drawers were seldom closed and it was the exception, rather than the rule, for anything to be hung in a closet. All neckties, socks, shirts, and BVDs were considered community property, which any of the three might wear. Suits and overcoats usually were borrowed only by special permission.

Since Doc was much stouter than Fred and Joe, his clothes were worn by them only in emergencies, when all their things were dirty. Doc, likewise, used their wardrobes only as a last resort, and then usually managed to rip their BVDs up the back.

There was very little bickering about who owned what clothes,

"ALTHOUGH YOU BELONG TO SOMEBODY ELSE, TO-NIGHT YOU
BELONG TO ME."

except in regard to tuxedoes. Doc had acquired his tuxedo before
he had put on much weight, so it was all but impossible to distin-
guish among the three tuxedo coats and trousers, not to mention
the hard-front shirts, collars, black ties, studs, patent-leather shoes,
and vests. The roommate who dressed first for a dance picked the
cleanest and newest of the garments, and the one who dressed
last usually had to tiptoe into some other room to swipe a clean
shirt or a pair of trousers which hadn't been slept in.

As for everyday laundry, each of the three was supposed to
mail his clothes home to be washed, but since no one wanted the
job of deciding whose dirty clothes were whose, never mind who
had got them dirty, they devised a system under which they took
turns sending home *all* the laundry.

The walls of their room were decorated with college pennants;
signs removed from streets, hotels, railroad cars, and, especially,
ladies' rest rooms; carefully made paddles reserved for initiations,

THE SUPREME SACRIFICE

Collegiate: I LOVE YOU SO, I WOULD LAY DOWN MY LIFE FOR YOU!
Flapper: YES, BUT WOULD YOU PULL UP YOUR SOCKS?

when pledges were required to assume the angle; invitations to various social events; and autographed pictures of wimmen.

The chairs, desks, dressers and beds were decorated with laundry, suits, overcoats, shaving equipment, towels, hair grease, halitosis medicine, hats, textbooks, one saxophone, three ukuleles, a mandolin, a banjo, and a complete set of traps which ran the gamut through drums of various sizes, gourds, cowbells, tambourines, and other sleep-disturbers.

There was also a table whose chief function was to support a wind-up phonograph and a few feet of records, mostly by Cliff Edwards, Ben Bernie, Paul Whiteman, Al Jolson, Gene Austin, Eddie Cantor, Ted Lewis, and Red Nichols and His Five Pennies. The phonograph could be muted, by closing a device at its front which resembled three slats from a Venetian blind, but no evidence is available that any of the three roommates ever made use of the device.

Customarily during the week, the three sophs assembled in their

Music
Down Through
the Ages

The College Chap
Days Gone by Played
the Swiss Zither

The Next Generation
Twanged the Spanish Mandolin
and Guitar

From Even Sunnier
Honolulu Came the
Uke.

From Sunny
California Came the
Hickman Whistle

Let Us Hope
That the Boys Won't Turn Next to
Scotland for Inspiration

"Just a Song at Twilight"

room after supper for a couple of hours of concentrated study. Immediately before exams, the cramming sessions might last for as long as four hours, during which time the roommates would advertise how hard they were working by wearing wet towels around their foreheads and sending out pledges for quantities of black coffee.

But almost always, whether the three were studying, cramming, shooting the bull, drinking, or simply listening to one of Doc's anatomical travelogues, the phonograph was kept busy.

Each of the three had his own ideas about how every musical number should be played. For that reason, it wasn't unusual for a calculus problem or a Horace ode to be briefly abandoned while one of the roommates grabbed an instrument or the drumsticks and helped Mr. Red Nichols or some other band leader through a difficult passage. Sometimes all three came to Mr. Nichols' assistance, first on instruments and then on a vocal refrain. Joe, by sliding the foot pedal and the bass drum over near his desk and by beating on the window with a drumstick in his left hand, found

At the University of Southern California
Senior: WHAT'S THE IDEA OF THE BIG DUNHILL DISPLAY?
Freshmen (as one man): WE'RE GOING DOWN TO GILDA GRAY'S HOUSE TO SEE IF SHE'LL REALLY STICK TO A FELLOW WHO SMOKES A PIPE.

The Equal Rights Theor

ould Work Both Ways.

that he could even help out while writing his themes. Doc occasionally dropped everything to leap into an elephantine, teeth-jarring clog step which caused Fred and Joe hastily to move ink-wells and ashtrays from the edges of the desks.

Some records were more likely to interrupt studies than others, but there was one record which was positively guaranteed always to bring all homework to a complete, grinding stop. None of the roommates ever gave a helping hand on their instruments to that record, either.

The piece was by a new singer and orchestra leader, Rudy Toody. Rudy had first made his reputation as a band leader while he was a student at an Eastern college. Now he was a top box-office attraction, and his records were selling by the thousands.

Rudy had a new style of singing, if you wanted to call it that. It was soft and dreamy, only nasal, and the women thought it was the cat's meow. Joe and his roommates, on the other hand, thought that any cat which meowed like that should be ashamed of itself and had better have its adenoids removed.

Whenever Mr. Toody's voice emerged from the phonograph, the roommate who had selected the record would pretend that he had done so by accident.

"How did *that* get on there?" he'd grumble. "I'd like to turn that guy's damper down."

Then all three would threaten to break the record. But the fact was that, however much they criticized Mr. Toody, they were fascinated by this new style of singing which they referred to sneeringly as "crooning."

For some reason that is difficult to explain, the three detested Rudy. It wasn't only his voice they detested. They detested *him*.

Perhaps they could have forgiven him if he were not so close to their own age, if he had not himself been a college man, and if the women were not so enraptured by him.

They could not cite these facts as the reasons for their dislike of the young singer, because the facts smacked so obviously of

Love Confessions

WHY DID SHE? in this issue

John Held Jr

THE THINKER

With the Coming of the New Year

We
bid farewell
to the
Flapper and the
Finale Hopper

But

We have with us
the
Gravy Haters
The Cake Eater
and the
Bun Dusters

by
John Held, Jr.

"Hello, Rudopho! Got time to give us a hair cut?"

jealousy. But they could, and did, cite other facts, or at any rate allegations.

"He closes his eyes when he sings," Joe was fond of proclaiming. "That's something else he ought to be shot for. I don't say it's not all right to close your eyes if you're singing to a sleepy-time gal in a rumble seat or something, provided it's dark out, and I mean dark enough to develop pictures. But he does it under a spotlight and before a whole theater full of people. And suppose the people get the idea that all college men are like that!"

"What burns me," said Doc, momentarily diverted from his favorite subject, "is that he holds a megaphone up to his mouth, but all the noise seems to come out of his nose. Waah, waah, waah — like that."

"Everyone in his right mind," nodded Fred, "knows that when a man's singing jazz he's supposed to sing like a man. He's supposed to sing, well . . ."

"Dew-acker-dew-acker-dew," sang Joe, accompanying himself by hitting a couple of chords on his uke.

"That's right," Fred agreed.

"Or, voe-doe-dee-oh," sang Doc, strumming *his* uke.

"Sure," said Fred. "But not" — he pinched his nose to insure the correct nasal timbre and closed his eyes in mock ecstasy — "waah, waah, waah."

Yes, Rudy Toody's record was about the only thing that could make a real dent in their study hours, and destroy their concentration. So that was another thing they resented about Rudy. Because there was no doubt about it, studying was important. Aside from the matter of personal grades, there was the scholastic average of the fraternity house to be considered. If the average of the house fell below "C," the brothers would be denied certain social privileges, including the holding of the June house party. A fraternity which couldn't even hold a house party might as well close up shop and call itself a dormitory.

But Mr. Toody's record, while certainly causing a break in studying, didn't necessarily mean that the roommates would not eventually get back to their textbooks. Usually, after Rudy had been excoriated, someone would put a decent record on the phonograph. Then they would dig into their work, with Joe keeping time on the bass drum and the windowpane, Fred occasionally picking up his sax to take a couple of hot runs, and Doc breaking into a clog step from time to time or grabbing up his banjo when Mr. Nichols, Mr. Whiteman, and the others who didn't close their eyes needed a little friendly assistance.

CHAPTER 4

"ANOTHER THING the high schools don't teach these days," Alfred continued, "is manners. Remember those delinquent monsters we sat behind at that movie a couple of weeks ago?"

"The musical?" Betty asked.

"The musical!"

"They were fairly noisy, all right."

"They just ruined the show, that's all. Every time that thin fellow sang, the girls screamed and the boys booed and stamped their feet. And when I tried to point out to them, as politely as I knew how, that they ought to have a little consideration for other people who had come there to try to enjoy themselves, they told me to, 'Hold it, Clyde,' and to 'DDT and TB.' What do those letters stand for, anyway?"

"I asked Richard about it later," Betty smiled. "I'm afraid that what they stand for is 'Drop Dead Twice and Turn Blue.'"

Shortly after the Christmas holidays, Rudy Toody and his Collegiate Vagabonds started on their first cross-country tour. One of their appearances was to be at a Chicago theater. Chicago was only a hundred miles or so from Midwestern, and the three roommates planned to be there.

The university had a ban against students' keeping automobiles at college, because an alarming number of sheiks, tea hounds, drugstore cowboys, lounge lizards, and other species of male undergraduates had run their flivvers into telephone poles during previous years. Also, some members of the Board of Regents seemed to be of the opinion that rumble seats had been designed deliberately to undermine the chastity of coeds. Obviously, regents who held this opinion had never themselves ridden in a rumble, because if there was anything that a rumble was designed deliberately to *prevent* it was the undermining of *anybody's* chastity.

In view of the automobile ban, the roommates planned to go to Chicago by train. Even if it had meant walking barefoot all the way, they had no intention of missing Rudy.

Not that they liked Rudy, they kept assuring each other. As far as they were concerned, Rudy won both the fleece-lined bathtub and the crocheted bicycle. Still, he undeniably had something that the wimmen went for, and they wanted to find out exactly what it was.

Doc thought of backing out, when he found that both Fred and Joe planned to take dates to Chicago, and that Betty Coed had got a blind date for him. Dates made Doc nervous and tongue-tied, and he avoided them whenever he could. But in this case it would have meant not only missing Rudy but also admitting that girls, except those who crossed their legs at a safe distance, terrified him.

The three sheiks and three flappers — all wearing raccoons and open galoshes — boarded a daycoach at Midwestern Junction at 5 P.M. They took the two front seats and the side seat at the head of the car. Doc did his best to edge away as far as possible from his date, but he took up so much room himself that he couldn't edge very far without landing in the aisle.

The roommates had brought their flasks, ukuleles, and kazoos, to while away the trip. The flasks were produced almost immediately, and passed around. Doc seemed a little more at ease after his drink, which had been a big one. Betty, who was sitting with Joe on the side-seat, crossed her legs and Doc leaned over to re-tie his shoe.

"I have on light purple bloomers and a white brassiere which, for your information, is killing me," Betty told him not unkindly, and without uncrossing. "If you're going to spend the evening tying your shoes every time one of us makes a move, you won't be

¶ John Held, Jr., *did this.*

exactly the life of the party. Sit up now and behave yourself."

Doc straightened up hurriedly, and this time almost *did* fall into the aisle. He fished out his flask again, took a long drink, waited a moment or two, and took another. When he brought the flask down that time, it was empty.

It took three drinks to bring Doc's courage around girls up to what was considered par for the average sheik.

WHAT ARE LITTLE BOYS MADE OF?

Snipes and snails
and raccoons' tails,
That's what little boys are made of.

But—

What are Little Girls made of?

To do this properly we must start at the foundation

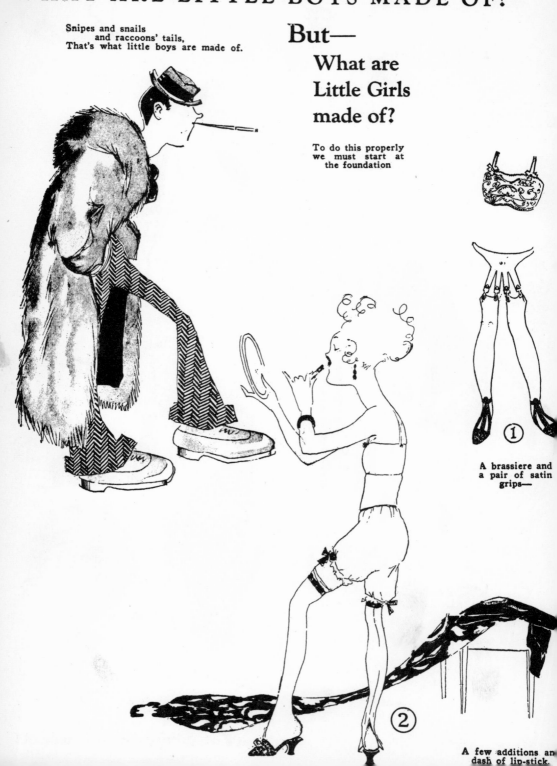

① A brassiere and a pair of satin grips—

② A few additions an dash of lip-stick

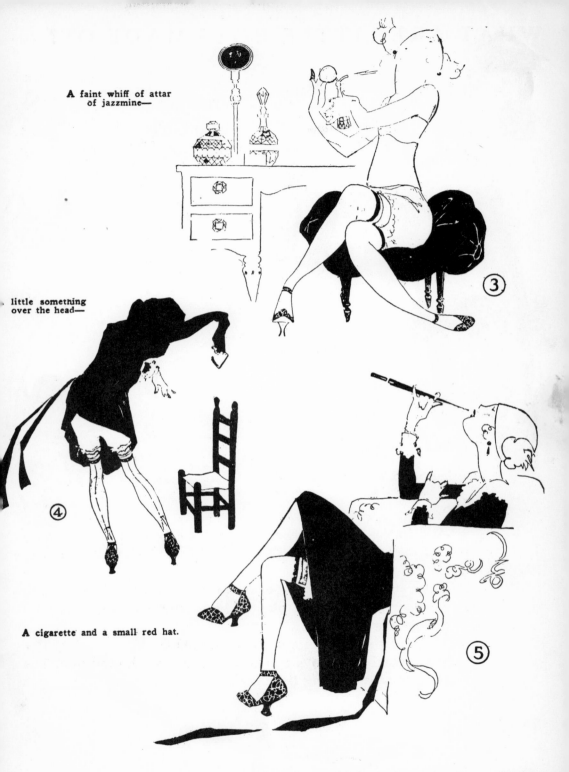

A faint whiff of attar
of jazzmine—

little something
over the head—

A cigarette and a small red hat.

—and that's what little girls are made of!

"BILL! SHE'S GOT *two* SETS OF GARTERS ON!"
"SURE, THEY'RE ALL WEARING 'EM NOW—ONE PAIR TO HOLD UP THEIR STOCKINGS AND THE OTHER TO HOLD UP TRAFFIC."

"And for your information," he said, easily now, "I have on a pair of Joe's BVDs which, although split up the back, are killing *me*."

"Don't you go drowning your sorrows just because the girls have on bloomers," Joe warned him, and the other passengers seemed to be enjoying the scene.

"She *says* she's got on bloomers," said Doc.

Betty raised her skirt a couple of inches and showed him. The passengers were craning their necks.

"Me, too, only mine are pink," said Doc's date. "Don't you go saying that I didn't have a blessed stitch on under my dress."

"Somebody's been doing a lot of talking behind my back," Doc complained.

"Pink, too," said Fred's date. "Don't go saying I didn't, either."

They showed him, and pink was right. Doc didn't seem particularly disappointed.

"Two pinks and a purple," he nodded. "Will one of you blabbermouth roommates of mine lend me a flask?"

"Don't you go getting yourself plastered," Joe warned him again. "You know what my old man said he'd do if I got arrested."

"Joe's been on his good behavior ever since the Feds arrested Betty and him," Fred explained to his date. "If he gets arrested again, his old man's going to make him go to work."

"You poor guy," she sympathized with Joe. "You mean if you ever get arrested again in college, you have to go to work? That's cruel!"

"The old man's not *that* unreasonable," Joe defended his father. "It's not forever. Just this semester. He and I have an agreement — not more than one arrest a semester."

Fred produced his flask and they all had a small drink. Then Doc hit a couple of chords on his ukulele, and Joe and Fred joined in on theirs, accompanying themselves on their kazoos. The kazoo, for those who just came in, is a small metal horn which, when hummed through, produces the sound-effect of tissue paper on a comb. In the hands of experts, such as the three roommates, the kazoo also can be made to sound like a muted trumpet.

They played the one about "Crazy Words, Crazy Tune, He'll be Drivin' Me Crazy Soon." The girls sang the chorus — "He sits around, all night long. Same old words to every song. Voe-doe-dee-oh, voe-doe-doe-dee-oh-doe."

Pretty soon a number of other people in the coach were singing, too.

Doc offered Joe's flask to a couple of old boys who were sitting behind him, and they had a drink. Then one of the old boys opened a suitcase and produced a quart of Golden Wedding — at least that's what the label said. All rye seemed to be Golden Wedding. It wasn't long before the quart was circulating among other passengers, and after half an hour or so a number of quarts had made their appearance throughout the coach.

Although smoking wasn't permitted, most of the passengers had lighted up. What had been a dignified assemblage when the six Midwestern students boarded the car was soon a noisy, smoky glee club of bosom friends. Even those who weren't drinking joined in on some of the songs, and shouted requests for numbers to the three college boys with the ukes and kazoos.

A conductor came in tried to enforce the no-smoking rule, but couldn't get any place and was completely drowned out by "Muddy Water." Doc offered the conductor a drink from somebody's bottle. The conductor said that since he was on duty he really shouldn't, but that he might take just a little nip. It turned out that the conductor had a fine bass, in spite of the fact that he was a chain-smoker.

It was suppertime when the train reached Chicago, but the six collegians decided to forgo eating and to devote the time instead to visiting a speakeasy. All of them except Doc were reasonably sober, and Doc was not unreasonably plastered. They took a cab to the theater, where they picked up tickets to Rudy's late performance, and then walked to the speakeasy district.

The boys each had a wide variety of speakeasy cards. Just as the social standing of a fraternity was judged in part by its bootleggers, so was the social standing of individual members judged in part by their speakeasy cards. It was customary to carry the cards in one's wallet, and while it was considered socially correct for a college boy's wallet frequently to be without money, it was considered socially incorrect for the wallet to be without an assortment of cards to Pierre's Place, Percy's Puff Palace, Louis' Grill and so forth.

Extra Fare

Now that the longer skirts are permanent.
What, oh, what, is to be done?
by John Held, Jr.

There is always a convenient
mud puddle or

We can be deliber-
ate or else

Discard the skirt entirely

But a sitting posture will always
suffice

If Pierre, Percy or Louis actually recognized a patron, and
called him by name, the patron was established as a man about
town.

The cards really weren't of much assistance in getting into a
speak. In the first place, the chances were that Pierre's Place had
changed hands and names several times since the cards were
printed. In the second place, since most of the Feds had cards,
you could get into a speak just about as easily without a card as
with one.

College boys, with their raccoon and porkpie trademark, usually
were admitted without question, providing they were behaving
themselves. College boys who were strumming ukuleles and singing their alma mater were something else again.

Consequently, the three roommates and their dates were on
their best behavior as they walked down a flight of steps into an
unlighted basement vestibule at what was, or used to be, Pierre's
Place.

"Keep the ukes under your coats," Joe warned, "and let me do
the talking. They know me here. Doc, stand up straight!"

Joe rang a bell. A light flashed on, and a peephole opened in
the door.

"Yeah?" said the peephole.

"Pierre?" asked Joe. "You remember me. I'm Joe College. I was
here last spring. I've got a card."

He held up the card. The door swung open and they walked
into a lighted hallway, barred by another locked door. Admission
to the hallway didn't necessarily mean admission to the speak. It
was simply that the man at the peephole, who was stationed in
the hallway, didn't want people hanging around the outside of the
place.

He was a flat-nosed thug in a tuxedo.

"You remember me, don't you, Pierre?" asked Joe.

"You don't remember me," grated the doorman. "I ain't Pierre."

"Well, Pierre will remember me, if you'll ask him to come out."

What is sauce for the gander

"Pierre don't live here any more. This is Tony's Place."

"You'll let us in, won't you?" Joe smiled his most engaging smile. "I'm an old-timer here, back when Pierre had the joint."

The doorman had spotted half of Doc's ukulele, poking out from under the raccoon, and decided in the negative.

"This ain't no speak no more," he said. "This here is a private home."

"Listen, we're all right," Joe argued. "Were all down here from Midwestern U. We're not Feds, honest."

is apple-sauce for the goose.

"You sure had me fooled," the doorman said. "You sure don't look like no college kids. I thought you was Andy Volstead hisself, and his vice squad. Sorry. Private home."

Then Betty took over, rolling her eyes and letting her coat drop open so the thug could get a good look at her legs.

"You remember me, don't you, Daddy?" she purred, twisting her hips. "I've never been here, but I'll bet you remember *me*."

"Maybe I do," he admitted. "If you was by yourself, I would. Especially since you ain't got no ukulele like the fat boy has got."

"The fat boy," Doc announced pleasantly, handing his ukulele to his date and preparing to take off his raccoon, "is going to beat the hell out of the next dumb bunny who calls him a fat boy."

"Keep your shirt on, fat boy," grinned the doorman. "And don't call me no rabbit."

"The gentlemen," Betty promised, "will check their ukes at the door. Since we've got tickets for the Rudy Toody show in a couple of hours, we won't be staying long enough to do any damage. Okay, Daddy?"

"Okay, Peaches," agreed the doorman. "Yeah, I guess I remember you. Now you guys leave them things with me, like Peaches said. And let one of youse start hollering about boola, boola and how you love deah old Harvard — and it's good night, sweetheart, for the bunch of youse. That goes double for you, fat boy!"

He pressed a buzzer and the inner door opened.

"Is my father in there?" Doc giggled in a falsetto.

"Get away from those swinging doors," Fred replied faithfully.

"I want a pretzel," giggled Doc.

"I oughtta have my head examined," complained the doorman. "Okay, now, give me them coed-coaxers, like you promised."

The boys were disarmed of their ukes, and the doorman patted their coats and pockets to see if there were any hidden saxophones, trumpets, or drums. When he felt the kazoos, he fished for them and produced them in triumph.

"Carrying concealed weapons, eh?" he gloated. "A bunch of you cowboys was in here last weekend with them things, and we had to call the riot squad. I'll check these, too."

The speakeasy had dim, pink lights, a horseshoe bar with a brass rail, three plug-ugly bartenders, and some booths. Since it was still early in the evening, the place wasn't very crowded or very drunk.

The six students stood at the bar. In order to show savoir faire, each was careful to put one of his galoshes on the rail and to hook an elbow over the rim of the mahogany counter.

The Girl Who Sat at the Ritz Without Showing Her Knees

Speakeasy habitues always liked college kids. It seems that a good many of the habitues once had been college kids themselves. Some had even gone to Midwestern.

"There isn't anything like the good times at college, is there? . . . And, kids, you want to enjoy yourselves while you can, because these are the best years of your life. I know you don't believe that now, but wait until you're as old as I am and have been through the School of Hard Knocks . . . And, name your poison, kids, because this one is on me . . . And put that stuff back in your pockets, because they don't take Confederate money here . . . And is old Wendy Wendell still in the Philosophy Department? I'll never forget once when old Wendy . . . And I don't suppose you kids ever heard about the time back in oughty-nine when we painted a horse red, white and blue and led it . . . And you mean to tell me this little skinny sheik is Joe College, the kid who beat Michigan? Why, I was there, boy, I was there . . . And bottoms up, everybody, because the next one is on me . . . And just between you and me and the gatepost, I'll be worth a cool million if the stock market . . ."

The girls had sidecars and the boys boilermakers — beer and rye. Then the girls had pink ladies and the boys Tom Collinses. They were all going to try Scotch and sodas, when Betty looked at the time and discovered they'd have to hurry to get to the theater.

The doorman helped them on with their coats and gave the boys their ukuleles and kazoos.

"Didn't we behave ourselves?" Betty asked him.

"Not a boola," he granted. "And nobody died for that Alma What's-her-name, neither. I give you credit."

"Thanks for the buggy ride," beamed Doc.

"You'll know us next time, won't you?" said Joe. "You'd better give us new cards, to be sure."

He gave them cards, and said they'd be hard to forget. But all of them knew the chances were that next time it would be somebody else's place, with a different thug for a doorman, and that no one there would have heard of Tony.

The cold air outside felt good. They were not experiencing any pain, and Doc was stewed, but still not to the eyebrows. They walked six abreast, with their arms around each other's waists and their galoshes flapping in cadence, down the sidewalk toward the theater.

"How does that boola-boola song go, anyway?" Betty tittered.

Fred started the song, and they drank her down, down, down for good old Yale. Then, still singing, they hail all hailed old Purdue, hit the line for Harvard, and, of course, let it be known that the Midwestern big team would do or die, boys, or know the reason why, boys.

Joe, Fred, and Doc hid their ukuleles as they filed, silent at last and on their best behavior, into the vast theater. The curtain was rising as they took their seats up front, only a few rows from the stage.

Rudy's band was wearing white flannel trousers (white flannel trousers really were yellow) with twenty-four-inch cuffs, and heavy, crimson sweaters, each adorned with a large green "T," presumably for Toody. Doubtless all members of the Collegiate Vagabonds were collegians, but if so some of them, who appeared to be in their fifties, must have been either repeating their studies or taking post-graduate work for thirty years or more. Some of them, also, looked a great deal more like vagabonds than collegians. All members of the band who *had* hair wore it college-boy style, plastered down and parted in the middle.

The band was arranged in three tiers on the stage. The pianist, drummer, bass fiddler, and girl vocalist were on the first row, the sax and banjo players were on the second, and the trumpeters and trombonists were on top.

The bass drum, which had a flashing light inside, was decorated for some obscure reason with a scene from a South Sea island. All other decorations on the stage were of college motif. There were

THE PHI BETA KAPPA STUDENT'S CAR

a goal post, a live bulldog wearing a blanket labeled "T," a battered Model T Ford with wisecracks painted on it, and a few hundred pennants. The girl vocalist wore a boyish bob, and her "it" was accentuated by a flat-chested, low-waisted flapper-type dress, the skirt of which didn't extend very far below the low waist.

There was no immediate sign of Rudy.

The drummer, who wore his mouth half open as if he were perpetually panting through it, hit two sharp licks against the rim of his snare drum, and the band exploded into "Baby Face." They played it through once with everybody sitting down, and then they played it through again with first the top row standing up and then the top row sitting down while the middle row stood up.

Finally, as they started to play it a third time, the spotlight picked out the girl vocalist. She skipped over to the piano, vaulted to the top of it like Helen Morgan, sat down, and took up the chorus.

"Did you see that," Doc called across four of his companions to Joe. "She doesn't have a blessed stitch . . ."

"Hush," warned Betty.

"Okay, Peaches," Doc mumbled resentfully.

The girl vocalist did "Baby Face" sweet and hot, and for an encore did "Gimme a Little Kiss, Will Ya, Huh?" in boop-boop-a-doop style. She was good and so was the band, but what the crowd had come for was Rudy, and it was getting a little restless.

Being primarily a showman, Rudy had delayed his entrance purposely. He also had carefully coached his band not to get *really* hot until he made his appearance.

Now the drummer hunched over his snare — shoulders crowding his ears and elbows crowding his shoulders — and beat a mad ruffle, while the entire band arose and the trumpeters, waving silver derby hats in front of their instruments, sounded off with flourishes and fanfares.

The spotlight shifted to one of the wings, and the great man made his entrance. He was a picture of nonchalance in an expensive raccoon which swept the boards and a porkpie worn almost on the back of his neck. The band struck up "Collegiate."

The applause and the screams of delighted females were deafening. But Rudy didn't acknowledge them. He stifled a bored yawn and lighted a tailor-made.

The girl singer slid off the piano — Doc's date clapped a gagging hand over his mouth — and helped Rudy out of his raccoon. Rudy also tossed her his porkpie, without looking at her, and then lounged to the front of his band.

Each member of the band produced a large pennant on a stick and a small megaphone.

"Yea, Rudy," they hollered. "Yea, yea, Rudy."

The cheer brought Rudy out of his trance, as if he were just

Collegiate, No End
What the 23-4 term will bring
by John Held, Jr.

Several new angles on "crashing the gate"

Beer and cigars is the new course

The ability to wear a waistcoat regardless of the temperature of the place

A few new ideas on "cutting in"

awakening to the fact that he was in a theater and had a band to
lead. He jumped to attention, facing the band. Slowly, he rose on
his tiptoes, and at the same time he raised his right hand, fore-
finger extended, above his head. Then, sharply, he brought the
finger down and pointed it rigidly at his drummer. The drummer
started a slow rhythm — pup-puppa-pa-pup-pup, pup-puppa-pa-
pup-pup. Rudy, his back still to the audience — picked up the
rhythm in his toes, his knees, his shoulders. Then he swung the
finger to the right, and the whole band burst into "Lonesome and
Sorry."

It was the bee's knees, and it was really hot, now. When it was
going just right, Mr. Toody turned to the audience for the first
time, shrugged as if to indicate that the band didn't need him, and
broke into a boyish grin. There was no denying that he was handsome and young-looking, in his blue-and-white-striped blazer and
pearl-gray flannels with spats to match. A soprano sigh went up
from the audience, in which even the three Midwestern coeds
joined.

And then came Rudy's vocal. The girl singer handed him a
large megaphone, with his initials on it, and he walked almost
apologetically to the footlights. A baby-blue spotlight followed
him, and the band muted down until it was honey-sweet.

Rudy closed his eyes and raised the megaphone. He sang softly,
intimately, as if he were reclining in the stern of a drifting canoe,
with one hand languidly trailing in the phosphorescent water, and
wanted someone in the bow to slide back and keep him company.
It wasn't dew-acker-dew or voe-doe-dee-oh. It was, and there's
no gainsaying it, waah, waah, waah.

The women and most of the men, too, were eating it up. Doc
was stoically silent while Rudy was lonesome and sorry because
someone had gone away. But when Rudy got to the part about
nighttime coming stealing, and put one hand over his heart while
the spotlight changed to purple, Doc thought it was high time
someone rocked the canoe. He picked up his uke from the floor,

thumped a chord, and started singing the way everyone knew a man ought to sing.

Doc was lonesome and sorry, yes, but he wasn't going to snivel about it, or whisper, or close his eyes in pain. He was lonesome and sorry at the top of his voice, with the proper amount of gravel in it, and you got the idea that if the mama who had gone away didn't promptly return to her senses, she was going to get mighty short shrift.

Fred and Joe, unwilling to let Doc carry the load all by himself, fished under their seats for their ukes and joined in. The three girls, who had been enjoying Rudy, decided that whatever damage was going to be done had already been done. They started singing too.

It wasn't bad, really. The six were hot, and they knew it. They drowned out Rudy completely.

Mr. Toody opened his eyes, and he wasn't pleased. Neither was the overwhelmingly large majority of the audience, which started demanding quite noisily that the sextet be thrown out. One middle-aged woman in the balcony kept recommending hysterically that they be lynched.

But there was a small minority of youthful male dissenters in the crowd who didn't like waah, waah, waah singing either, and they joined in with the Midwestern sextet.

Ushers started dashing down the aisle to eject the six, who also were being forcibly pushed out of their seats by irate women in their immediate vicinity. Three uniformed policemen, blowing their whistles, were on the ushers' heels. Rudy, with his eyes wide open and snapping, kept demanding through the megaphone that the six wise up, shut up, sell out, and act their age.

Joe decided he wouldn't give his right name, but he knew he was a gonner and would have to go to work, if they took his fingerprints. The worst of it was that he also knew the six of them were in the wrong and had made jackasses of themselves. But of course they couldn't have let Doc take the rap by himself, and that waah,

waah, waah *was* a little too much to take on an empty stomach.

Rudy made a quick recovery. Perhaps he remembered his own college days, or perhaps he wanted to keep to a minimum any publicity about the disturbance. At any rate, he motioned to his drummer for a ruffle. While the drummer was hunching and ruffling, Rudy held up his hand for the audience to give him quiet, and finally he got it.

"Don't kick them out and don't arrest them," he grinned. "I always have trouble with college boys. In Detroit it was grapefruit I got."

The crowd gave him a round of applause for his magnanimous action, and Joe joined in enthusiastically.

"I guess somebody must have smelled a cork, eh?" Rudy chuckled. It was apparent that he was pleased with the way this ad-lib part of the program was turning out. The audience giggled. Joe, who was ready to swallow anything within reason providing it would keep him out of jail, nodded sheepishly.

"Where are you six from, anyway?" Rudy asked conversationally.

"We're from Mid . . .," Joe began. But Doc was on his feet.

"Vassar," Doc hollered. "And you know what I wish?"

"No," said Rudy, who wasn't quite so pleased as formerly with the ad-libs, "what do you wish?"

"I wish I had a crate of grapefruit," Doc announced.

"We'll go quietly," Joe promised the policemen who were reaching for them.

Joe led the way up the aisle with the other five following in single file. Some women in the audience told him that he should be ashamed of himself and some were booing, but there were a few cheers, too. Doc brought up the rear, with an exaggerated lock step and an occasional clog, while playing the "Prisoner's Song" on his kazoo and ukulele.

"Even so," Rudy shouted to the police through his megaphone, "don't lock them up."

Joe decided that Rudy was a pretty good guy after all. As they left the theatre, amid threats from the police about what would happen to them if they got in any further trouble, Rudy's singing could be heard again. It was amazing how his voice carried. He was back in the canoe again.

CHAPTER 5

"PERHAPS I could excuse the younger generation for its zipper morals and terrible manners," said Mr. College, "if occasionally some member of that generation would give me credit for as much as a grain of sense. Richard brings a crowd of them here after a dance, for a ten-course Roman banquet that he describes as a snack, and when they see me, what happens?"

"They surely don't tell you to hit the road, toad, or to go to bed, Fred," smiled Betty.

"Not in so many words. But I'm talking about their treating me as a blithering idiot. When they see me, they start telling each other how refreshing and tangy the gingerale was at the dance. And at the same time, they start popping life-savers, chewing gum, and sen-sen into their mouths, when they think I'm not looking. And then they quickly light cigarettes. I'm supposed to be too stupid even to have the faintest suspicion that perhaps they may have had something stronger to drink than gingerale."

The June house party always started on a Friday and continued through Sunday. The brothers moved out of their rooms early Friday morning and into nearby rooming houses. Thus the second, bedroom, floor of the fraternity could be turned over to the girls who arrived shortly after lunch. Most of the girls came from out of town but a few, like Betty Coed, were students at Midwestern and simply moved for the weekend from their sorority houses into the fraternity house.

Some alumnus and his wife also moved into the house Friday, to act as chaperones and to be sure that the brothers steered clear of the second floor. The chaperones were selected more carefully than any of the individual dates. The ideal chaperones were amiable, broadminded, heavy-drinking, near-sighted, slightly deaf, wearers of squeaky shoes. Of course it was all but impossible to find an alumnus and spouse both of whom met all these specifications. But the brothers annually spent a great deal of time searching for a couple which came as close to the ideal as possible. While it was true that no couple had ever accepted more than one invitation to chaperone a party at the house, it was equally true that very few couples had ever been tendered more than one invitation.

There was a legend in the fraternity, which may or may not have been based on fact, about an unfortunate brother of a few years before. It seems that, during his senior year, he had finished his final exams and gone to Chicago for a three-day toot. He returned somewhat bleary-eyed to Midwestern on a Saturday afternoon. Forgetting that a house party was in progress, he had gone to his room, taken off his clothes, and walked down the hall to the central bathroom.

The bathroom contained three toilets, eight sinks, and six showers. The showers were in a community stall within the bathroom and separated from the rest of the room by marble partitions and a canvas curtain.

The house party participants had been away on a picnic when the senior arrived at the fraternity, so he didn't bump into any of the girls as he paraded down the hall, naked except for a towel tossed carelessly over his shoulder.

"The trouble with you boys to-day is you have no imagination!"
"Well, girlie, nowadays we don't need imagination."

But the picnic ended a few minutes after his arrival, and the
girls trooped upstairs to dress for dinner. A good many of them
made a bee line for the bathroom, and most of them planned
showers before slipping into their evening dresses.

Through the restful hiss of a hot shower, which was beginning
to restore his nerves to something approaching normal, the senior
had heard unmistakably female voices. His first reaction was to
turn off the shower, while he planned an indignant protest to the
House Committee. Girls weren't supposed to be upstairs, except
on football weekends when rules were relaxed to allow some
privacy for drinking. Things had come, the senior thought, to both
a pretty pass and fine howdy-do.

With the shower hiss extinguished, it became frighteningly
apparent that the girls were not only upstairs, but in the bathroom.
From the babble of voices and high-pitched giggles, there seemed
to be a good many of them.

He tiptoed over to the curtain, pushed it aside about a sixteenth
of an inch, and finally mustered the courage to peek out. There
were ten girls within the range of his vision, in various stages of
undress, and more of them seemed to be arriving every minute.
Some girls were obviously preparing to come into the community
shower and one girl was completely prepared. Some of them, too,
were discussing the various brothers and the fraternity itself, in
uncomplimentary terms, and some were chatting about subjects
that no gentlemen would have listened to, if he could help it.

The senior stared a moment, fascinated, and then flinched away
from the curtain. He knew he was trapped. The only exit was
through the bathroom, which was completely out of the question.
And he couldn't stay where he was unless he was prepared to play
host, within a matter of minutes, to a showerful of undressed
females.

It required some quick thinking, but at first all he could do was
stand there and sweat. In desperation, he turned on his shower
again, faced the wall, tried to cover himself with lather, and

Why

At a Fraternity Dance There Are Always Too Many Girls---

That

While at a Sorority Hop There Is Always a Big Stag Line?

prayed that he might himself pass as a female. All the time, though, he knew it wasn't going to work and that he'd be discovered. And then, to make matters worse, he dropped the soap.

"Hey, how's the water in there?" one of the girls called gaily. "You sure must have got out of your picnic things in a hurry."

"Save some hot water for us," another girl shouted.

He groped for the soap. He saw the shower curtain move as the girls prepared to enter.

Then he had a flash of genius. All men looked pretty much alike below the neck. It was just their faces which were different and by which they could be distinguished.

His towel was hanging on a hook within the shower enclosure. He grabbed it and, as the curtain was thrown open, wrapped it completely around his face and head.

The shrieks of the undressed flappers, as they backed away from the entrance to the shower enclosure, were deafening. But with considerable dignity and thorough knowledge of the floor plan, the turbaned and masked senior walked through the girls to the door of the bathroom.

"If you ladies will excuse me," he said as he turned toward them and bowed gallantly, before making a deliberate exit from the bathroom, "I hope to see a good deal more of you before the party's over."

Then, with head still wrapped, he walked sedately down the corridor, felt his way down the stairs, got an overcoat from the downstairs closet, dropped his towel, and ran across the street to borrow some clothes from the brothers of a fraternity where there wasn't any house party.

Maybe it was a legend, but all the brothers of Joe College's day certainly believed it. They even embellished it with an unlikely story about how one of the girls had hollered that she could swear the man wasn't her date; and how another had hollered that *she* could swear he wasn't even a member of the fraternity.

In Joe's day, it is doubtful that any brother, however bleary-

eyed, could have forgotten about house party weekend. Because everyone looked forward to it for months, and preparations for it started weeks in advance.

Also there was the matter of cleaning the upstairs rooms, which in the case of Joe, Fred and Doc, was a project requiring several days. Such a project, once completed, was about as liable to be forgot by its participants as Hercules was liable to forget his comparable chore of the Augean stables. Indeed, Hercules in some respects had an easier job than the roommates. He at least had a river to divert and there is no record that he had to struggle with a bass drum and other noise-making impedimenta.

"I DIDN'T CARE MUCH FOR TRIXIE—HER NECK WAS TOO LONG."
"CAN'T AGREE WITH YOU THERE, OLD MAN; I ENJOYED EVERY MINUTE OF IT."

¶ What the correct young man will try to wear, by **John Held, Jr.**

Additionally, almost all of the furniture had to be moved out of the downstairs, to provide plenty of dancing space; a bandstand had to be erected; Japanese lanterns strung; and the floors waxed. The pledges did most of the dirty work downstairs, but no brother returning from a bender in Chicago or any place else could possibly overlook the change in the appearance of the house. If he did overlook it, he'd better watch out for his neck, for he might hang himself in the spider web of crepe-paper streamers which extended from the front hall up the stairs to the second floor.

Although stags from other fraternities were invited to the house party dances, all of the brothers and pledges were supposed to attend the dances with dates. Experience had demonstrated that the bonds of brotherhood — however sworn annually in blood in

the secret and sacred chapter room — sometimes dissolved dis-
astrously, also in blood, when a stag brother stole the house party
date of a non-stag brother.

The rule about dates posed somewhat of a dilemma for Doc,
whose experiences on the Rudy Toody expedition had failed to
lessen his fear of girls. There certainly was little danger that Doc
would try to steal anyone's date, and even less danger that he
would have succeeded. However, Doc couldn't bring himself to
ask that the rule be waived for him, on those grounds.

Doc finally solved the dilemma by inviting his sister, who was a
freshman at Confederate College for Young Ladies, in Alabama,
to attend the party as his date. Doc's family was from Pittsburgh,
but his mother had been born in Alabama and had retained
very definite ideas about the education and rearing of young
women.

The sister's name was Margie, and according to Doc she was an
extremely inexperienced and naive girl—not at all like the Midwestern flappers. Doc kept reminding the brothers that they
weren't supposed to act like sheiks with Margie. No one was to
offer her a cigarette, since she didn't smoke, and anyone who
spiked her drinks would have to reckon directly with Doc. Since
she attended an institute which catered exclusively to females,
Doc pointed out, she didn't know very much about college boys.
Presumably, although Doc didn't say so, Margie wore not only
bloomers but flannel pantaloons.

No one paid much attention to Doc's warnings and threats.
They felt sure that any sister of his would be fat, big-bosomed,
tongue-tied with the opposite sex, and homely. They didn't propose to act like sheiks or anything else, except possibly absentees,
in the immediate vicinity of Margie.

It would be pleasant to record that Margie surprised them all
by turning out to be a slender, flat-chested, glib-tongued, beau-
tiful mama, of the red-hot variety, with a sparkling personality
and fast habits.

SHE LEFT
HOME UNDER
A CLOUD

Fortunately for the sake of our story, that happened to be precisely the case.

Margie was petite, blond, and loaded with "it." Perhaps she didn't smoke at home. But the first thing she asked for, when Doc led her into the living room of the fraternity Friday afternoon, was a cigarette. She asked for it even before Doc had a chance to introduce her around, and it was immediately apparent that Margie needed no introduction. She made friends quickly.

"How about you, Ole Hotshot?" she asked Joe, in a honey-dripping if adopted Southern drawl. "Have you got a coffin nail for li'l old me?"

She walked over to a davenport where Joe was sitting with Betty. She produced a foot-long cigarette holder and nonchalantly put it between her teeth. She leaned over and deliberately re-rolled her stockings, thus calling attention to her marvelous legs and bare, dimpled knees. There were about fifteen couples in the room. All of the men, excepting Doc but including Joe, practically had their tongues hanging out.

"A'm gonna call you Ole Hotshot," she told Joe, raising her eyes slowly to meet his, and then batting her eyelashes. "Ole Hot for short. Okay, Ole Hot?"

"Gee, sure," croaked Joe. Then, regaining some of his poise, he added: "You bet your sweet life, honey chile."

"How about a cigarette, Ole Hot?"

"You won't get one from me," Joe grinned. "I've been fully instructed about corrupting children."

Somewhat to the disapproval of Betty, Margie bounced into Joe's lap, ran a hand down his cheek, across his chin, and up the other cheek.

"Do you think of me as a child?" she asked throatily, wriggling in his lap and throwing her legs over the arm of the davenport, thus furnishing the assembled brothers with fairly positive proof that the flannel pantaloons were a figment of somebody's imagination.

"Not any more," conceded Joe, who found her an extremely attractive lapful.

"You get up from there," Doc ordered. Then, when that command got no results, he pleaded, "If you get up, Margie, *I'll* give you a cigarette."

"I'll give you a whole pack," Betty said dryly.

It seemed that all the brothers, too, were quite eager to give Margie a cigarette. She finally chucked Joe under the chin, bounced out of his lap, and accepted a cigarette from a senior and a light from a junior. Then she inhaled, blew smoke in Doc's face, and sat down on the floor.

"Ah don' know why, but ah always like to sit on the floor," she explained.

A number of brothers quickly brought her cushions, and seemed to enjoy tucking them around her. She paid little apparent attention to them, but busied herself rolling her stockings again, and broke into a song entitled, "Roll 'Em, Girlies, Roll 'Em." She was the life of the party, which frankly had been dragging a little before her arrival, and she knew it.

"Ah'll bet ah look a fright," she said, opening a vanity case and applying lipstick.

Five or six of the brothers assured her that, on the contrary, she looked like a knockout.

"Mah pin," she squealed, discovering the pin in the vanity case. "Ah almost forget about you Yankee men."

She pinned it on her shoulder, and the brothers crowded around to see what it had to do with Yankees. There was some writing on it which, on close examination, stated, "If you can read this, you're too damned close."

"She was only," winked Margie, "the farmer's daughter, but she know her oats."

The brothers thought that was exceptionally funny. Their dates didn't appear to be particularly amused.

"You're really a hot number, Margie," Fred told her.

"Ah'm a hot potato," Margie admitted, clicking her tongue twice, "and hard to cool. She was only the artilleryman's daughter, but she had a caisson me."

"I think," Doc said miserably, "I need a drink."

"That's mah bubber, mah *heavy* date," Margie giggled. "Doc, Ah'll bet you've got a bottle hidden away that's right off the boat. *Scraped* off." She clicked her tongue twice.

"Scraped off," echoed the brothers, roaring with laughter and slapping their thighs.

"She was only Joe Miller's daughter," mumbled Betty, "and I think I need what Doc says he needs."

"No drinking until after the dean calls," Joe warned her and Doc.

Margie wondered if anyone felt like dancing with li'l old her.

"You know us wimmen," she said, "we want to eat our cake and have our cake eaters, too."

Almost all the brothers volunteered their services. Someone turned on a phonograph, and a number of them helped Margie to her feet. But instead of picking any individual partner, she broke into a Charleston in which ten or twelve brothers joined. Then, unwilling to share the spotlight, Margie demonstrated for them a new dance that was all the rage down in Ole Alabam, entitled the Sensation Stomp.

The other girls, meanwhile, sat disapprovingly around the edge of the room. Doc flushed with embarrassment, as Margie kicked up her legs and made her arms go in sweeping circles while she licked first her right thumb and then her left thumb and then shouted "hotcha-cha," followed by two tongue clicks in rapid succession. The tongue clicks, incidentally, were like the sound you make when you want a horse to giddap.

Joe, who had an important question he intended to pop to Betty sometime during the house party, was among the few boys who had kept their chairs.

When the record was finished, Doc ended the Charleston and

¶ From the look in his eyes and the look of his clothes he was dressed to kill.

Sensation Stomp session by putting on a slow waltz. A number of brothers again offered their services as a partner to Margie, but she skipped over to Joe.

"Come on, Ole Hotshot," she drawled. "You wouldn't give me a cigarette, but now you got to dance with me."

"But I haven't danced with my date yet," Joe protested half-heartedly, while practically leaping to his feet.

Margie told him he had all night to dance with his date, and slid into his arms. She stood on tiptoe to put her cheek against his, and clung to him octopus-fashion all the way down to the tips of his shoes. Joe tried to hold her away, at first, because he could see over her shoulder that Betty didn't appear very enthusiastic about the performance. But Margie danced like an angel, and gradually his arm tightened around her waist.

"She was only the photographer's daughter," Margie confided, "but she was well developed. Right?"

"You're darned tootin'," Joe conceded. He closed his eyes and danced.

"There's going to be a moon tonight, Ole Hot," Margie whispered in his ear.

"I'll bet," Joe stalled, also whispering, "you know every detail of it by heart."

"Ah do not, either," Margie protested. "But Ah'll bet you could help me memorize it."

"You've got a pretty smooth line," said Joe, still noncommittal.

"When Ah call a man Ole Hot," Margie told him, "it's not a line. Ah'm sincere."

The record ended, and Joe opened his eyes. Margie turned him loose, after a soul-searching look into his eyes, and he drifted over to pick up Betty, who had been dancing the last part of the record with Fred. Someone wound the phonograph and changed the record, but Betty held Joe at arm's length as they started to foxtrot.

"Gee, it wasn't my fault," Joe finally said. "I didn't ask her."

"Who said you did? Besides, you don't think I care, do you?"

"You saw her come over and get me."

"And you bounced up as if there were springs in your back. And then you went to sleep in her arms. Did you have a nice nap?"

"Don't be like that, Baby," Joe begged. "I've got to be polite to my roommate's sister, don't I?"

Imitating Margie, Betty threw both her arms around Joe's neck and glued herself to him.

"Ole Hot," she panted grotesquely into his ear, "there's going to be a moon tonight."

Joe stopped dancing, and pushed Betty away so that he could look at her. "How did you know about that?" he marveled. "She just barely whispered it."

"Don't worry," snapped Betty. "I can spot a female astronomer

"She Couldn't Tell a Lisle"

the minute one walks into the room and curls up in my date's lap."

Joe pulled her up close to him again, and resumed dancing.

"You're jealous," he teased. "And psychic."

"I'm not jealous. And I wish I were psychic enough to know what you told her when she started discussing astronomy."

"I didn't tell her anything," said Joe.

"That's what I thought," Betty snapped. "Well, there'll be plenty of visiting stags at the dance tonight. I guess I can manage to have a good time."

The record ended, and Betty left him and went over to sit by Fred's date. Fred and most of the brothers were kneeling on the floor around Margie, and someone had produced a pair of dice.

Joe decided that perhaps the house party wouldn't be a very good time, after all, to ask Betty that big question. He had to admit that Margie was a hot number all right, but Betty was something extra-special — the snake's hips. Joe stood by himself in a corner, moodily watching both Betty and the crap game. The brothers had been shooting for dollars, and finally it was Margie's turn with the dice.

"Ah'll shoot a nickel," she announced. "Who says Ah'm a faded blonde?"

"You're faded, Mama," said Fred. "I'm a plunger." He covered her nickel with five pennies.

Margie rattled the bones, kissed them, and threw them out on the rug. Joe knew without looking that it was going to be a seven or eleven, and apparently it was, because Margie announced triumphantly:

"Ahm a natural blonde, and now I'll shoot another nickel. What's sauce for the gander is apple-sauce for the goose." She clicked her tongue twice, rolled the dice, squealed happily, and let it be known that the shoe clerks had better get out because *this* time she was going to risk seven cents, on account of baby needed a new pair of moccasins.

After the crap game, the girls were coached carefully by the

The Faded Blonde

Punch Committee about the expected visit that night of the dean of students.

Fred, who majored in chemistry and thus was an acknowledged expert in the manufacture of bathtub gin, was chairman of the committee. He had appointed his two roommates as his assistants.

Fred explained to the girls that Old Dean Twitty, a widower, could be counted upon to arrive about nine-thirty and leave about ten-thirty, which seemed to be his bedtime.

The theory in inviting the dean was that, once he had seen for himself how orderly the party was, he would be apt to discount the complaints he was certain to receive about the conduct of the party after his departure.

"So you see," Fred continued, "there can't be any drinking until after Old Twit leaves. No necking, either."

"While the dean's here, we'll have a meeting of the bored," said Margie. "But after he's gone, Ah'm a dumbbell waitin' for exercise." She didn't forget the two tongue clicks, and once again the brothers roared appreciatively.

"We don't want a meeting of the bored," Joe put in. "We want

A MEETING OF THE BORED.

you gals to give the old boy a real rush. Treat him like he's a sheik
— you know. Keep cutting in on him, and tell him how gracefully
he bunny-hugs — or whatever that step of his is called. Make a
play for him, and impress him with what nice gals you are, so he
won't believe any of the lies he may hear about how we raised
hell."

"You can count on the Punch Committee taking care of the
punch," Fred announced for the benefit of the brothers, "*after*
Old Twit leaves. I don't say that what we've got is pre-war, but
it's smooth as silk."

"Not pre-war," giggled Margie. "Pro-war. A fight in every
drink."

"Good God," sighed Doc.

Actually, the best that could be said about the product manufactured by the Punch Committee was that it was pre-house party.
The committee had made it the day before.

The most important piece of equipment in the manufacture of
bathtub gin is, of course, a bathtub. Although the brothers relied
on showers for bathing, there was fortunately a bathtub in the
basement. The tub was used primarily to bathe the house mascot,
a great dane. When thoroughly scoured by the pledges, however,
the tub was also deemed adequate for gin manufacture.

Despite precautions taken by the medical school, one of the
graduate brothers who was studying medicine had managed to
obtained the alcohol for the gin. He was exceedingly vague as to
the precise source, within the school, of the alkie. It smelled fairly
smooth, however, and burned with a blue fame. Fred pronounced
it entirely satisfactory.

On the day before the party, the Punch Committee had poured
the alkie into the bathtub, added an equal amount of distilled
water and a considerably lesser amount of glycerine, juniper juice
and some other fluids whose identities were known only to Fred.
Fred measured each ingredient to the last cubic centimeter, using
beakers and retorts, and finally stirred the mixture with a carefully

sterilized glass rod. He also wore a rubber apron and had a Bunson burner handy, just in case he needed it.

When completed, the gin was siphoned from the tub into bottles which had been collected during the year from the brothers' wastebaskets. The members of the Punch Committee had been on the wagon Thursday, in preparation for the house party. But in the siphoning process, some of the gin inevitably got into their mouths, and they pronounced it exceptionally good stuff. They were particularly pleased that they had made certain of its purity by using distilled water and by sterilizing the glass rod.

The Friday night dance was a fashionable affair, and the sheiks and flappers dressed carefully for it.

Most of the girls had shingle bobs, which didn't require much attention in the back but took a lot of fixing in the front and on the sides. One thin curl, clinging tightly to the forehead, was supposed to come down almost to the bridge of the nose and then head back up again. Similar curls, one on each side, emerged forward of the ears and partially circled the cheeks.

Eyebrows were plucked to a pencil line, and mascara was daubed on so that individual eyelashes were grouped together into five or six king-sized, up-swept spikes. Lipstick was applied in a cupid's bow, almost as high as it was wide.

The girls' formal dresses were short and filmy, decorated around the neck with fringe that hung down to a similar row of fringe around the hips. As if this wasn't enough of an entangling alliance, the girls also sported ropes of shell-like beads which looped twice around their necks and still had enough slack to dangle to their thighs. Stockings, of course, were rolled below the knees.

The boys were clad, at either extreme, in a layer of Stacomb and black socks which sagged messily into patent-leather shoes. Their tuxedoes featured bell-bottom trousers with wide stripes up the sides, white, double-breasted vests; and black, butterfly ties that they had helped one another to tie.

The formal supper Friday was served at seven-thirty. Two hours later, the orchestra and the dean arrived simultaneously.

The girls clustered around the dean, helping him off with his coat, straightening his black string tie, brushing imaginary lint off his spotless coat-tails. The dean dapperly adjusted his pince-nez, which hung from a black ribbon around his neck, and seemed to be enjoying himself. Betty picked a pink rose from her corsage and pinned it to his lapel.

The band was a five-piece outfit imported from Chicago. It had come to Midwestern by bus that morning and had played that afternoon at a dignified, non-alcoholic faculty tea dance. Lugging their instruments tiredly but gamely, the musicians plodded through the front hall of the fraternity. Then, spying the vat-sized punch bowl which the Punch Committee had provided, the band members dropped their instruments and lurched forward like desert prospectors in sight of an oasis.

The bowl contained an inky, tee-totaling mixture, bubbling evilly, which consisted of grape juice and gingerale. Floating limply on the surface were browning slices of banana. Nevertheless, the band members dived in hopefully with punch glasses, toasted each other silently, and drank.

The effect was dramatic. One band member was seized with a violent fit of coughing. Another, stealing the line from Mr. W. C. Fields, inquired loudly and indignantly as to the identity of the saboteur who had spiked the grape juice with grape juice. A third, with his glass empty and his cheeks extended, looked around furtively as if for a potted plant. The other two loudly demanded something alcoholic for a chaser.

When nothing alcoholic was forthcoming, they proceeded glumly to the bandstand, where they jerked the covers off their instruments, tuned them viciously, and struck up a half-hearted waltz.

The girls led Dean Twitty to the punch, and he sampled it and pronounced it both delicious and refreshing. The girls sampled it, too, and said that if there was anything they were crazy about, it was gingerale and grape juice, flavored with bananas. Dean Twitty said yes, we have no bananas, and the girls practically knocked themselves out laughing at this witticism. The dean also said that he liked the punch so well he thought he'd have another glass. Joe, Fred, and Doc watched the performance with obvious approval.

Finally Betty told the dean she had heard what a smooth dancer he was, and that while she supposed it wasn't very lady-like for a girl to ask a fellow — well, a gentleman, but of course Betty really thought of him as a fellow, at a time like this — to dance, she wondered if . . .

And of course the dean said he would consider it a great honor and a great pleasure. Holding her at arm's length, he started with determined gaiety, tempered with professorial dignity, to crouch, take two running steps, leap, and then crouch again. This was his idea of how modern dancing, such as the Charleston and Black Bottom, was performed. Frankly, he thought he was pretty good at it, too.

One by one the other girls cut in, and finally it was Margie's turn. Joe watched her from the stag line, and caught occasional snatches of the conversation. Margie's drawl had never been more Southern. She had never dreamed that anyone up no'th, particularly a dean, knew all the latest dance steps. Somehow or other, Margie had mastered his crouch, run and leap, and executed it gracefully. She even managed to work in something where she kicked her legs up during the leap and Dean Twitty, not to be outdone, was following suit.

Noticing Joe's pleased smile of approval, Margie suggested rather coyly, when the music stopped, that she and the dean wander out on the porch to look at the moon. Unfortunately, Joe missed that portion of the conversation.

Teaching Old Dogs New Tricks

A SERIOUS HISTORICAL STUDY

"ON WITH THE DANCE"

BY JOHN H

We will start with the time when the coryphée danced to the pipes of Pan.

Then came the stately minuet,

The two wicked round dances, the waltz and two-step with detachable cuffs.

And now we tune up the radio and get the one about Bananas and Jazz, Godhelpus!

Dean Twitty's field was astronomy, and he was more than delighted to find a pleasant youngster with what seemed to be a real interest in celestial bodies. The idea, consequently, seemed like a corker to him.

"It's a little chilly for me to be out there without my topcoat," he told Margie. "But I'd be delighted to get a little air. And as a matter of fact Jupiter should be putting on a real show tonight, too. Suppose I get my coat and meet you on the porch."

But the dean's conversation was lost to the Punch Committee, since the orchestra had sulkily struck up a loud foxtrot. All that Joe, Doc, and Fred noted was that it was ten-thirty, and that Old Twit was getting his topcoat and departing through the front door.

The Punch Committee rushed to the kitchen, emerged with four quarts of gin, and added them to the punchbowl. There was an immediate run on the bowl, with the orchestra in the forefront. When the music was resumed, it was neither spiritless nor sulky.

It was about that time that the dean, having shown his attractive companion not only the moon and Jupiter but forty or fifty other stars, returned to the party. Although it was considerably past his bedtime, he had no intention of departing until he had formally thanked his hosts for an enjoyable evening and bid good night to the young ladies who had been kind enough to dance with him.

The Punch Committee intercepted him and Margie at the door.

"It was mighty good of you to come, sir," Joe told him, "and we *do* wish you didn't always have to leave our parties so early."

The dean consulted his watch.

"My goodness," he exclaimed, "I really do have to go. I just thought I'd say goodbye to you gentlemen and the ladies."

He pushed past them to the dance floor, and circulated around bidding good night to those who weren't dancing. The girls, recognizing their duty, gathered quickly around him in a protecting circle. But despite their efforts, his wanderings ended at the punchbowl.

"It's been a charming party," the dean said. "I should be on my way. But first I believe I'll have just one more glass of this delicious punch."

"I don't believe it's cold, sir," Joe stammered, backing up to the punchbowl and throwing out his arms. "Let me get you a cold glass from the kitchen."

"No, indeed," said the dean. "This will do nicely."

He ducked agilely under one of Joe's arms, picked up a glass, and took the dipper from the bowl. Betty grabbed his hands.

"How about one more dance, dean?" she asked.

Dean Twitty shook his head.

"Then at least let me take your glass into the kitchen and get some cold punch, sir," Betty begged.

"You're all too kind to an old man," smiled Old Twit, who seemed really touched. "I do have to go, though, and this punch will do quite nicely."

The Bee's Knees

He pulled his hands gently but firmly from Betty's, and he filled his glass.

"What is it you say?" he chuckled, determined to be one of the boys. "Here's mud on you?"

"That's close enough," Joe groaned.

The dean drank. He must have discovered, at the first sip, that the punch was practically straight gin. Perhaps he knew, even before the first sip, why they had been so determined to get his punch from the kitchen. But his expression didn't change, and he finished the whole glass, bottoms up, without removing it from his lips.

"Extremely refreshing," he nodded. "Good night, everybody. It has been a great pleasure."

He bowed and walked sedately through the front door, which four or five brothers were eagerly holding open for him. After he had disappeared, the brothers heard a dismaying thump, as something hit the sidewalk. Joe rushed out to see if assistance were needed.

"It's all right, son," the dean chuckled. "You don't need to worry about me — that really wasn't the first drink I've ever had. I dropped my walking stick, but I've found it. Good night."

As the dean, swinging his stick, walked jauntily down the sidewalk in the bright moonlight, Joe thought he heard Old Twit click his tongue twice, the way a man does when he wants a horse to giddap.

The Trophy Room
"Killed 'em on my last trip to Canada."

CHAPTER 6

"You know and I know," said Mr. College, "that the opposite sexes have been mutually attracted ever since Adam and Eve raised Cain."

"How true, how true," Betty humored him, walking over to his chair and running her fingers through his thinning hair.

"But this new generation," Alfred continued, "is convinced that it *discovered* that attraction. Richard thinks that you and I — and all previous generations — simply don't know what we've been missing. He's actually sorry for us. He doesn't believe there's ever been a generation, before his, which held hands in a darkened theater, or sneaked a kiss in the vestibule when the parents weren't looking, or generally mauled each other when the opportunity arose."

"Mauled each other?" Betty asked with mock indignity, pecking him on the forehead. "As I recall, you were the one who did most of the mauling. I practically had to beat you off with a club. For my part, I . . ."

It was three o'clock in the morning. As in the song, Betty and Joe had danced the whole night through — but not very often with each other.

After Dean Twitty's departure, the music and the dancing had progressively picked up. Betty was avoiding Joe. Whenever he had broken on her, she had winked at someone she knew in the stag line, who had cut before Joe could dance more than three or four steps.

Betty always got a rush from the stags, but Joe was well aware that tonight she was purposely giving him the brush-off.

The result had been that Joe had made somewhat of a spectacle of himself. During almost every intermission, and in fact whenever the drummer got up to visit the punch bowl, Joe had taken over the traps. He was quite expert at them, as a matter of fact. He could throw the sticks up into the air and catch them. He could put the sticks in his teeth and, tossing his head up and down, beat a roll on the snare drum. And he could get up from the drummer's chair and leap like a chimpanzee around the bandstand while he pounded out rhythm with the sticks on the piano top, on the music stand of the saxophonist, on the planks of the stand itself, and, on one occasion, upon the skull of the band leader.

The orchestra members, being old hands at playing for college boys, took Joe's performance in stride. The leader even went so

"MARGE PULLS AN AWFUL LINE."
"YEAH? WHAT'S HER LINE?"
"OH, YOU KNOW—THAT SINCERITY STUFF."

"LIFE IS LIKE THAT!"

far as to tell Joe that if he needed a job after graduation, to be sure to look him up.

Joe also had danced one high-kicking Charleston with Margie. They had brought the dance off with such success that the other couples had formed a ring around them and clapped hands to the rhythm. At the end of the number, the other couples demanded an encore, and Joe and Margie had done a snaky tango.

"Know who you remind me of, Ole Hot?" Margie had whispered during the tango. "Rudolph Valentino." Then, with a sigh, she added: "Wonder if the li'l ole moon is still out there?"

"You ought to know," Joe pointed out. "I saw you and Fred sneak out to check on it, about twenty minutes ago."

"Ain't Ah the limit?" Margie giggled. "She was only a sailor's daughter but how she could luff."

Joe had been careful not to accept this or other previous invitations from Margie to indulge in outdoor moonshine. Also, he had been sure to keep his eyes wide open during the tango. Joe still had hopes of getting back into Betty's good graces. He felt sure that if he disappeared for even thirty seconds with Margie, or closed his eyes while dancing even for a cat nap, those hopes would explode.

Margie, incidentally, had got even a bigger rush from the stag line than Betty. A number of the stags, and even some of the brothers, also seemed intent on loading Doc with spiked punch. They'd throw their arms around his shoulders and lead him toward the bowl. But Doc was staying sober enough to patrol regularly the porch, the garden, and the darkened library, whenever Margie disappeared from the floor.

Margie had been the life of the party, all right, and had repeatedly strutted her stuff.

She was wearing purple crepe de chine, cut round and high at the neck and ending two inches above her knees. The matching purple fringe around her hips was long enough to give the effect of a hula skirt. A large, artificial peony, worn halfway between her right hip and backbone, bobbed in and out of the fringe when she walked.

Margie had climbed up on the piano to sing several songs with the orchestra — including one number, entitled "It's Tight Like That," that received calls for three encores.

She had borrowed a bearskin coat and derby hat from one of the brothers, pushed her stockings down around her pumps, and sung "Collegiate" — "very, very, seldom in a hurry, never ever worry, we're collegiate, rah, rah, rah!"

She had done a shimmy in the middle of the dance floor, making the purple fringe tremble, the necklace clatter, and the peony undulate, while the stags whooped and hollered advice about how she should "shake that thing."

And she had dashed up to her room, during one intermission, to reappear carrying a pair of hiking boots and a bottle of poison ivy medicine. Of course the boys wanted to know why the paraphernalia, and Margie explained it was her motoring equipment — the boots in case she decided to walk home, and the poison ivy medicine in case she didn't. No one had a car at Midwestern, but the joke seemed to go over well, just the same.

Joe had been stuck only once — with the plump, tittering, perspiring date of one of the pledges. Joe had ended up with her after a Paul Jones. Perspiring himself, and with his usually glib line gone slack, Joe had pushed her up and down the stag line, mutely appealing for succor. He was too much of a gentleman to do as some brothers occasionally did — hold a dollar bill in the hand which encircled an unwelcome partner. He wasn't rescued until there was another Paul Jones, and his temper wasn't improved any by the fact that Betty wore a self-satisfied smirk whenever she breezed by him in the arms of constantly changing partners.

And so it was three o'clock, Saturday morning, and Joe finally decided to get things straightened out with Betty. He cut in on her, and before she could wink at any of her friends in the stag

John Held Jr

line he twirled her a couple of times and pulled her into the pitch-
dark library.

"Let's sit down awhile," he pleaded. "I want to talk to you."

"Are you going to behave yourself?"

"Aw, you know me, Betty."

"That's why I'm asking, Ole Shot."

"Certainly I'm going to behave myself, and if you want to call me anything, call me Rudolph Valentino. That's my new name."

"Oh, it's tight like that and shake that thing," mimicked Betty.

Joe took her hand and they groped their way across the library. They started to sit on a davenport, but they found another couple there and the couple was taking up all the room. They tried an overstuffed chair, and again found it occupied. A second davenport also was occupied, but Joe lit a match and found out that the occupants were a freshman and his date.

"Beat it, kids," he ordered. "Davenports are for upper classmen."

¶*By that old back seat engraver,*
John Held, Jr.

¶ *Steamheat and southern exposure by* John Held, Jr., *a scene paintin' rascal*

"Even during house parties?" grumbled the freshman's date. "My cow!"

"Especially during house parties," Joe told her. "Go outside or someplace."

"But every time we go outside," complained the freshman, "Doc comes snooping around looking for his sister. He's worse than the chaperones."

"Try the kitchen, then," Joe suggested. "Or the basement. But davenports are . . ."

"Okay, keep your shirt on," said the freshman. "Come on, baby."

The couple departed, and Joe and Betty sat down. Joe put his arm around her shoulders, but she sat up straight and wouldn't lean toward him.

"You seem to know all the places for necking," she pouted. "Outside, the kitchen, the basement — you must have had a busy freshman year."

"Don't be like that, baby. You wouldn't want a daddy who wasn't experienced, would you?"

Betty admitted that she guessed she wouldn't — that she liked daddies who had been around; who had gone places and done things.

"You're the one I burn for," Joe whispered. "You know I didn't give Margie a tumble."

"No," Betty conceded. "I've been watching you, and I guess you didn't."

"I've had the blues all night, because of the way you've been treating me," Joe said. He tightened his arm, and she leaned her head against his. Joe rubbed her hair and she rubbed her face across his chin. Joe slowly turned her face around, to see whether she'd let him kiss her. She didn't turn her face away, so he did what he was supposed to.

It was part of the game for a boy boldly to see how far he could go. And it was also part of the game — although many parents of the era refused to believe it — for the girl to see that the boy did not go too far.

"Let's stretch out and be comfortable," Joe suggested cagily. "I'm tired from all that dancing, aren't you?"

"You know I don't neck horizontally," Betty reproved him. "If I necked horizontally, you wouldn't respect me any more."

"I would too," Joe protested. "I don't mean with everyone, but if you necked horizontally just with me I'd respect you, all right. And besides, this is a house party, isn't it?"

"Just the same," said Betty, "a girl's got to think of her rep."

Joe kissed her again, this time a good deal longer than before, and finally Betty had to push him away.

The Dance-Mad Younger Set

"Boy," she panted, "you sure know how to kiss."

"So do you," Joe conceded, also panting. "Who's been giving you lessons?"

"You wouldn't want a mama who wasn't experienced, would you?" Betty mimicked.

They kissed again, and they rubbed cheeks, and then Betty sat in his lap and they kissed again.

"If my mother," said Betty, "could see me now!"

"The old folks just don't understand," Joe agreed. "Times have changed, that's all. We're not living in the Gay Nineties any more."

"Thank goodness," Betty sighed. "You may kiss my hand, sir."

Joe kissed her — not on the hand. But when he started trying to explore, and when he mentioned again how tired he was from dancing, Betty quickly redrew the line.

"I'm not that kind of a girl," she whispered.

Secretly, Joe was glad she wasn't that kind of a girl.

"I've got something I want to ask you," he told her. "I've been planning to ask you for a long time, but then when you got sore about Margie I didn't know whether to ask you or not. But, anyway, what do you say we get married?"

"Permanently," Betty asked conversationally, "or companionate marriage?"

"I don't know. Which do you think?"

"Well, companionate seems to be all the rage. It's the modern thing to do. I don't know, though . . ."

"Neither do I," said Joe. "Maybe I'm old fashioned, but if you and I get married, I think I'd rather have it permanently."

"So would I," Betty whispered. "I guess I'm old fashioned, too. But what would we live on, Joe?"

Joe thought that over. "I suppose my old man would cut off my allowance," he conceded. "Say! How about *your* old man?"

"I'm afraid he'd cut off my allowance, too," said Betty.

"I guess we'd better wait until we graduate, then."

"I guess so, too."

"But we can be engaged, if you want to wear my fraternity pin."

They kissed again, and then Joe fastened the pin to her dress.

"It's really a solemn occasion," he told her. "Just think — engaged!"

"Does that mean you won't go out with any other girls?" Betty asked.

"Does it mean you won't go out with any other boys?"

They agreed that the occasion, while solemn, didn't need to be quite *that* solemn. Joe also pointed out that, now they were engaged and in view of the fact that he was tired out from dancing, there shouldn't be any objection to their reclining and relaxing on the davenport.

"It's naughty, but it's nice," he pleaded.

But Betty shook her head.

"Nice girls," she said, "only pet vertically."

They kissed again.

"Just think," said Joe. "Mrs. Joe College. How does that sound?"

"It sounds fine," Betty admitted dreamily.

"When we're married," Joe sighed, "we can sit on the davenport every night with the lights out."

In the other room, the band shifted from "Drifting and Dreaming" to "Just a Cottage Small by a Waterfall." Margie was rendering the vocal.

"She was only the Doctor's sister," said Betty, "but she was a pain in the neck to me. Besides, she's wrong about you and Valentino. To me, you're more the Lucky Lindbergh type."

CHAPTER 7

"IF THERE'S ANYTHING WRONG with Richard," Betty College said, "I think we're the ones to blame. Maybe he's a little spoiled, but . . ."

"A *little* spoiled," Alfred interrupted. "His slightest wish is our command. You can go ahead and accept the blame for it, if you want to, but I know he didn't get his mortal fear of work from my side of the family. He thinks that any job is an imposition, that any job requiring manual labor is a form of slavery."

Joe felt a heavy weight of responsibility, now that he was an engaged man. He was going to have to buckle down, and he was going to have to stop horsing around, and he was going to have to start facing up to things.

Of course all of that would come later, when he returned to Midwestern next fall. Meanwhile, three pleasant months of summer vacation were the immediate outlook. He knew he would miss Betty during those months, but they had promised to write each other every day.

Since Joe's grades had been satisfactory and since he hadn't been arrested lately, he anticipated a reasonably cordial reunion with his parents. Even though Betty wouldn't be there, he couldn't help but look forward to the summer of loafing, swimming, sailing, and tennis at his family's summer place on the shore.

He was particularly eager to get behind the wheel of his flivver again, to put his sloop in the water, and to see the old crowd which hung out at the beach and yacht club.

Joe wrote a ten-page letter to Betty, on the train going home.

Take a flat-chested maiden and youth in his first dinner coat.

Add a little heavy breathing.

ohn Held, Jr.

Mix thoroughly at a country club dance.

Allow to simmer in a parking space.

Garnish with orange blossoms and embarrassment and serve —for the rest of your life.

(It was a passionate declaration of his love, and a source of embarrassment to him during his married years, when Betty occasionally would produce it and read it aloud to him, with a nostalgic catch in her voice. Incidentally, since neither of them went in much for letter-writing, their correspondence that summer lapsed as if by mutual consent, after the exchange of three or four sticky epistles.)

Joe's parents met him at the station, and he was mighty glad to see them. His father had a new Franklin, and Joe was allowed to drive it home. It was a smooth-riding buggy, all right. It felt good to be driving a car again, after the autoless months at Midwestern.

Joe's mother thought he had filled out a good deal, and that his beard looked as heavy as his father's, and that he was handsomer than ever and probably had been breaking some poor girl's heart. She was convinced, though, that he hadn't been getting enough sleep or the right kind of food, and that he certainly was suffering from overwork.

Joe decided not to minimize his mother's impressions about physical exhaustion and overwork.

"When," he asked weakly as he wheeled the Franklin along, "do we leave for the shore? You don't know how I've been looking forward to it, during the last nerve-racking months of study, study, study — and then more study. And then the pressure of exams, one after another. It's a killing pace."

"Oh, dear," said his mother, almost in tears. "You poor boy. And you haven't heard yet what your father has decided."

"Study, grind, and exams," intoned Joe. "Exams, grind, and study. No wonder so many college students are committing suicide. There's been a regular wave of them."

"You poor boy," Mrs. College repeated. "Your father wouldn't listen to me."

"Wouldn't listen about what?" Joe asked suspiciously. "Study, grind, and exams."

"Alfred," said Mr. College, "you may fool your mother, but you don't fool me. You happen to have a good family background, so

The Speaker of the House

you get satisfactory grades, which is as it should be. And you get those grades with an absolute minimum of study, study, study — and then more study."

"Like fun!" Joe protested.

"Precisely," said Mr. College, who was so pleased with the remark that he decided to belabor it. "That's the trouble. You like fun. And if you are physically exhausted, it's not from study, grind, and exams or from the three in reverse order. It's from dancing, drinking, and diddl . . ."

"I won't allow that word," Mrs. College announced firmly.

"Dilly-dallying with coeds at that house party," Mr. College finished strongly.

Joe grinned in spite of himself, but the grin quickly vanished as

Mr. College continued. Mr. College was of the opinion that his son was now old enough to do some work in the summers, instead of lounging around like a lounge lizard and cake-walking around like a cake-eater. A summer job, Mr. College pointed out, would give him both self-reliance and experience, not to mention spending money.

"You mean," Joe gulped, almost ramming the Franklin into the back of an ice wagon, "after all I've been through trying to be a credit to you in the last nine months, you want me to go to *work?*"

"Look out," yelled Mr. College, grabbing the wheel.

"You shouldn't frighten the boy with talk about work, when he's driving the car," Mrs. College reproved her husband. "Do you want to kill us all?"

"Work!" moaned Joe. "You're kidding, aren't you, Pop?"

"No, I'm certainly not kidding. As I say, a job will give you experience and spending money."

"But I've already got plenty of experience and spending money. I don't need any more of those."

"Frankly," Mr. College told him evenly, "I don't know too much about your experience. I suspect it is along channels which neither your mother nor I would approve — probably the less said about your experience, the better. As for your spending money, it's time you learned just how hard I have to work for it."

Actually, Mr. College was the head of a large real-estate agency and was so successful that he hadn't done any strenuous work himself for ten or fifteen years. In his father's present mood, however, Joe thought it advisable not to point that out.

"For nine nerve-racking months," sighed Joe. "I've been walking the floor at night, worrying, cramming, laboring . . ."

"You sound like an expectant mother, not a man who's simply being asked to support himself for three short months," Mr. College exploded.

"That's the thanks I get for passing all my courses," Joe continued. "You want to turn me out in the street."

SHE CUTS HERSELF A PIECE OF CAKE.

PLUCKING THE EYEBROW.

LETTING OUT A HEM.

The Home Life of the Tennis Champ

An Old Man's Game

"I'm not turning you out on the street, I'm getting you a job at my office."

"It's such a nice office, dear," Mrs. College pointed out, patting Joe's hand. "And not very hard work."

"Of course," Joe's father said, "just because you're my son you can't expect to start at the top. You're going to have to win your spurs as I did."

"Your father won his spurs after grandfather died and left him the agency," Mrs. College nodded agreement.

"But if I work in the office, I can't go to the shore," Joe complained. "Do you mean that you and mother expect me to stay in

"Why are you leaving the party so early, Joe?"
"Oh, I've got to get the car home in time for dad to drive it to work."

the hot city and slave, while both of you are basking in the cool breezes at the shore?"

"It wasn't my idea," Mrs. College sniffled. "It was your father's."

"And how about the Commodore's Cup?" ask Joe. "You know I have two legs on it, and that if my boat wins this year I'll get permanent possession. Good night!"

"I reminded your father about the Commodore's Cup," Mrs. College sobbed. "He wouldn't listen to me."

"There are more important things in life," Mr. College pronounced slowly, trying to keep his temper, "than the Commodore's Cup. When I was your age, I didn't do any basking in the cool breezes at the shore. You can bet your sweet life on that."

There was one quite harmless remark that always could be counted upon to send Mr. College into a rage. Joe knew this full well, and employed the remark judiciously. He decided, however, that the occasion was ripe for the remark.

"Times have changed," he asserted smugly.

"Yes," said Mr. College, and his voice was quivering, "they have. They have changed to such an extent that children think they can defy their fathers."

"But I'm not a child," Joe pointed out.

"You're damned right you're not," Mr. College shouted. "You're old enough to support yourself. Your allowance stops as of this minute."

"Yes, sir," said Joe, who knew when his father had taken all he intended to take.

"There are millions of people in this country," Mr. College continued, still angry, "who can't afford to go to the shore in the summer and bask in the cool breezes."

"I know, sir."

"And from now on," hollered Mr. College, but not quite so loud as before, "you're one of them."

"Anything you say, sir," said Joe.

"That's better," his father told him sternly.

The All-Year-Round Girl

Joe parked the car in their driveway and toted in his bags. By the time he and his parents were seated in the living room, Joe judged that his father had cooled off enough so that it would be safe to reopen the subject.

"How much will you pay me, if I go to work in the office?" he finally asked.

"More than you're worth, Alfred," said his father, who obviously was pleased with the boy's apparent change in attitude. "More than you're worth, son."

"How much?" Joe insisted.

"I intend to be generous with you," Mr. College assured him magnanimously.

"How much?"

"Seventeen dollars a week." Mr. College rolled out the figure as as if it were a fine, fat, round number. "Of course that's considerably more than we usually pay youngsters who are just starting in. So I wouldn't want you to mention the figure around the office."

"Don't worry, sir, I wouldn't. I'd be just as much ashamed of it as you are."

Mr. College, now eager to establish a truce, attempted a hearty laugh. "You're a sharp bargainer," he said. "All right, twenty dollars a week. How does that sound?"

"It sounds," snapped Joe, "lousy. No thanks. I'll get my own job."

"Haw," pronounced Mr. College. "Doing what? Selling subscriptions to *Boys' Life*? Carrying ice like Red Grange? Collecting our war debts?"

"Nothing that hard. I want to make my money like some other people I know. Taking life easy."

"I like that!" bellowed his father. "After the way I've worked my fingers to the bone . . ."

Mrs. College was sobbing again. "I don't think it's right," she wheezed, "for you two to fight on the very first day of Alfred's vacation. We've been looking forward for months to his vacation, and . . ."

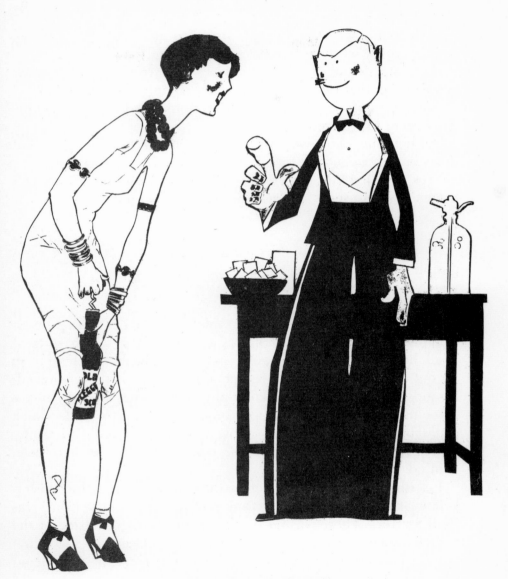

Pulling for Him

"Looking forward, huh!" snorted Mr. College.

"Vacation, huh!" snorted Joe.

Both males went over and comforted her, but Mr. College couldn't resist what he thought would be the last word.

"I'm sorry, dear," he told his wife. "The trouble is that some people think that twenty dollars is something to be sneezed at."

"I'm sorry, Mother," said Joe. "The trouble is that some people don't seem to realize that times have . . ."

"So help me," bellowed Mr. College, "if you tell me again that times have changed I'll take a strap to you, big as you are."

"Yes, sir," Joe said innocently. "What did I do wrong? Aren't I even allowed to speak around this house? Good night!"

Joe spent the next two days hanging around the drugstore, composing a one-page letter to Betty, and working on his Model T, which he soon had running in what was known as rattling good shape.

The Tin Lizzie was an ancient, topless touring car, with a brass-trimmed, steam-belching radiator; cushions from which tufts of black horsehair protruded; wooden-spoked wheels which were so far out of line that they swayed pendulum-wise as they revolved; a windshield that folded in half along a horizontal axis; no brakes — Joe used the reverse pedal as a brake; an exhaust whistle which could be heard all the way across town; and a red and white, zebra-striped body on which, of course, wisecracks had been painted.

Inscribed in green paint across the top of the radiator, with a yellow arrow pointing to the crank protruding from the front, was "Self Starter." There was no front door on the driver's side of the vehicle, since that was where Mr. Ford had placed the spare tire.

In order to start the car, Joe had to get in from the right hand side and adjust the handbrake, the switch, the spark, and the hand throttle. Then he got out again and cranked, while manipulating

A Poor Fish out of Water

by Sara Haardt

❡ *Sculped by that hardy old trail breaker* . . .
John Held, Jr.

a wire choke-loop which protruded from the radiator. If the spark had been adjusted correctly, there wasn't too big a chance that the crank would kick backwards and break his arm.

When the engine coughed, Joe had to race back into the car and re-adjust the spark and throttle. It was the rule, rather than the exception, for the engine to snort, wheeze, grunt, and finally expire before he could get from the crank to the spark.

There were three pedals on the floor — the foot brake, which didn't work; the reverse, which backed up the car and doubled for a brake; and the forward gear. There was no foot accelerator; if there had been, a person would have needed a third foot to operate it.

Signs painted on the body included "Chicken Here's Your Coupe," "Pardon My Dust," "Don't Laugh, Rolls-Royce, We're Sisters Underneath the Tin," "So's Your Old Man," "Bring Your Roller Skates, Mama," and "The Mayflower — Many a Little Puritan Came Across in It."

By the time the car was deemed to be in usable shape, Joe had exhausted the three dollars and seventeen cents that was left from the money his father had wired him to pay his train fare home from Midwestern, and the fifteen dollars that his mother had secretly given him from her household allowance. With debtors' prison practically staring him in the face, it was necessary to have another financial chat with his father. Joe tackled him after supper, while Mrs. College was in the kitchen helping the maid with the dishes.

"I guess I'll be ready to go to work tomorrow," Joe began.

"That's fine," his father boomed heartily. "I knew I wouldn't have to speak to you about it again."

"I'll need about fifty beans to get started. Can you spare it?"

"Thanks for the Buggy Ride"

"Fifty dollars!" neighed Mr. College. "Are you crazy, man? You already have all the clothes you need. Besides, you don't have to be slicked up at the agency. Nobody's going to notice you there. You'll be working vacation reliefs — first for the office boy, then for the janitor, and finally, if you're savvy enough, for the file clerks and telephone operator."

"I thought I told you," Joe explained patiently, "that I'm not going to work at the agency. I'm not interested in a menial job that only pays twenty beans a week."

"Then where," demanded Mr. College, "*do* you propose to work?"

"I don't know. Some place where the work is easy, and it's cool, and the pay is good, and where they don't expect a college man to substitute for the office boy."

"Maybe Mr. Rockefeller needs someone to run Standard Oil while he's away passing out dimes."

"That's a thought," Joe agreed. "But look, if you won't give me the fifty beans, how about *lending* them to me? I'll pay you back."

"When?" asked Mr. College. "And with what?"

"In a couple of weeks — and with the money I'm going to be making."

"You really think it grows on trees, don't you?" Mr. College said, shaking his head in disbelief. "You've never earned a nickel in your life, and you think all you have to do is snap your fingers and the stuff will start coming out of your ears."

"Oh, banana oil, I'm not a moron," Joe said. "I'm a Midwestern man. After all, you can't expect me to be happy working for peanuts."

"And I suppose that, when you get your Midwestern diploma, you'll expect to take my place as the head of the agency, for five hundred a week."

"Is that what you make?" Joe asked with some interest.

"Never you mind what I make."

"If that's what you make," Joe assured him, "it might do tempo-

DUMB ANIMALS

A few recent but not rare
discoveries

by John Held, Jr.

Drug storeus
cowboyus.

Equus asinus.

Marathonus dancerus.

Cloakus modelus.

rarily, until something better comes along. And, meanwhile . . ."

"All right," his father surrendered, reaching for his wallet. "And, meanwhile, I'll lend you fifty dollars. But it's the last cent you'll get out of me this summer, so you'd better make it stretch. When I was your age, I would have considered it a fortune."

"Thanks a lot, Pop," said Joe, ramming the bills carelessly into a pocket. "It seems like a fortune to me, too. But I suppose that when I get a job like yours, it'll seem like chicken feed."

CHAPTER 8

"KIDS TODAY," Alfred College told Betty, "have things too easy for their own good. I don't know what's got into the American people. The Chinese worship their ancestors, and the Americans have come to worship youth. No wonder we're raising a thoughtless generation of spoiled brats who haven't any sense of values. When I was a boy, my father made me sweat for everything I ever got. I remember one back-breaking summer, when . . ."

After negotiating the loan, Joe scribbled his parents a note that he was going job-hunting and might get in touch with them in a couple of weeks at their summer cottage.

Early the next morning, before his parents arose, he packed some clothes in his Tin Lizzie, propped up the note on the parlor mantel, and started for the shore.

He had to stop every twenty miles or so to fill the flivver's radiator and about every fifty miles to patch a tire or tinker with the spark coils. The cylinder head cracked from overheating when he was halfway to his destination, but a nice middle-aged couple who happened to be passing in a Jordan pushed him fifteen miles to the next town. They insisted on buying him lunch there, and then accommodated him further by pushing him to an automobile junk yard. Joe bought a cylinder head for a couple of dollars and installed it in a few minutes. While he was in the junk yard, he also swapped spark coils and radiators, which took about half an hour more. When he finally cranked the engine again, it ran — if not as good as new — at least as well as when he started from home.

Setting out again toward the shore, he drove until dark with only two more flat tires to repair. He bought his own supper and, since he didn't want any trouble with traffic cops, borrowed a red and two white lanterns from a road-construction job. He attached these to the Ford, whose own lights had ceased to function several years before, and pushed forward.

He reached the shore shortly before midnight, thankful that he had had no serious car trouble on the trip. When he checked into the best hotel there, he still had forty-five dollars left from his original fifty.

The next day he went about the task of seeking his fortune. There was no scarcity of jobs, so he could pick and choose as he pleased. Almost every hotel at the shore was looking for bus boys and waiters, but those jobs seemed a little too much like work to Joe. That wasn't the kind of fortune he was seeking.

The fact was that the fathers of a good many boys Joe's age — boys who as children had always come to the shore — had decided it was time their sons started to learn something about their businesses. Most of these boys had been put reluctantly to work in the city, after scenes not unlike the unnerving scenes recently enacted in the Colleges' house. As a result, there was a shortage of college boys at the resort. Good-looking, eligible college boys, who might be expected to attract girls to the various clubs and other places of entertainment, could write their own tickets.

In past summers, before he had been divorced from his allowance, Joe usually had spent the mornings at the beach, the afternoons sailing and playing tennis at the yacht club, and the evenings attending dances or picnics. He saw no valid reason for varying that entirely satisfactory routine.

Since he was an expert swimmer and well known at the shore bathhouse, he had little trouble landing a morning job as lifeguard at the beach.

Next he tacked up a sign on the yacht club bulletin board, offering his services to supervise picnics for private parties and also to give tennis and sailing lessons. The sign added that advanced sailing pupils might even have an opportunity, for a nominal extra charge, to crew for Joe when his sloop participated in the Commodore's Cup series of races.

And then he went to see Happy Ferdie, who was reorganizing his Melody Smoothies to play at the yacht club and hotel dances, and landed a job as drummer.

"He's not the hottest traps man in the world," Happy had confided to the rest of the Smoothies after Joe's audition, "but he's pretty fair. And the women will burn for him, I'll tell the world."

The sailing, tennis, and picnic jobs began to pour in. Most of Joe's pupils were girls whose mothers wanted them to get into the social swing. Some of the pupils were girls who wanted to meet Joe. And a few of the pupils were the mothers themselves. There were also a fairly large number of young children, whose parents wanted them out of the way during the cocktail hour, which at the shore started about two o'clock in the afternoon and continued for as long as the parents were able to maintain their perpendicular. Joe decided to give free sailing lessons to a couple of his college girl pupils, in return for their helping him take care of the children.

As for conducting picnics, Joe's service was the answer to many a shore-goer's prayer. With Joe cooking the clams and lobsters, entertaining the teen-aged daughters, and available to furnish the ukulele music for the group singing after the moon came up, the

In the game of tennis, its
not so much the overhand,
as it is the underthings.

by John Held, Jr.

official host could devote himself exclusively to the mixture, distribution to the adults, and personal consumption, of cocktails.

Within a day or two, Joe was back in his regular summer routine — beach, sailing, tennis, dances, picnics. But now he was getting paid for it — handsomely paid, too. His time was almost immediately booked solidly for July and reservations were coming in for August. He added two more college girl assistants to his afternoon staff of kindergarten teachers.

Mr. and Mrs. College, meanwhile, were becoming genuinely concerned about their son's whereabouts and welfare. It was true, as Joe had pointed out, that there had been a wave of student suicides, which the newspapers were attributing to the "bitter disillusionment of the Jazz Age generation."

Even Mrs. College, who blamed her husband for Joe's disappearance, had to admit that the boy did not seem to be exactly the bitterly disillusioned type. But her theories as to his whereabouts ran the gamut from a soup kitchen in the Bowery to a Godforsaken outpost of the French Foreign Legion. She saw Joe as a tattered, shuffling figure cadging nickels from passers-by. She saw Joe, with his nose pressed against a restaurant window, gaping at a chef making hotcakes. She saw Joe in striped prison garb, serving a ten-year sentence for having broken into a grocery store and too proud to let his parents know of his desperate plight. All of these situations seemed less improbable to Mrs. College than the possibility that her son had actually taken a job.

Mr. College, at first, skeptically expressed the view that the boy would show up when the fifty dollars had been spent. However, after the first week passed without word from Joe, Mr. College became as worried as his wife. He still scoffed at her fears about the Foreign Legion. But, at the same time, he knew that a week was about all the mileage Joe ever got out of fifty dollars.

By the time Mr. and Mrs. College arrived at their summer cottage, they were so jittery and upset that they weren't speaking to each other. In fact they wouldn't even have been able to agree to leave the city together, in the first place, if Joe's note hadn't said he might get in touch with them at the shore.

They were immensely relieved, therefore, to hear the hellish sound of an approaching exhaust whistle, just as they sat down to supper a few hours after their arrival at the cottage. As the whistle came closer, and was punctuated by a series of backfires, Mr. and Mrs. College were sure it was Joe's Model T. Both of them raced to the door.

The Model T skidded to a stop. Joe switched off the motor, and nonchalantly leaped out. The engine was steaming, and it back-fired twice more, rocking the chassis, before it finally died.

"My boy, my boy," wept Mrs. College, running down the front steps and smothering her son in her arms.

"Hi, folks," Joe grinned. "Gee, it's good to see you. Everything been going hunky-dory? Have I got any mail?"

"You look all right, Alfred," Mrs. College said anxiously. "I'm glad to see you so nice and tanned. You haven't been going hungry, have you? He doesn't *look* as if he had joined the Foreign Legion or anything, does he, dear?"

"No," Mr. College agreed darkly. "He looks as if he's been loafing around the beach and eating regularly on credit. Well, I won't have it, do you understand, Alfred? I said you had to support yourself this summer, and I meant exactly what I said."

"We can talk about that later," Mrs. College pronounced firmly. "Right now, it's time for supper, and I intend to see that the poor boy gets at least one good meal."

"I'll be glad to pay for it," Joe assured his father. "A home-cooked meal would taste mighty good, though."

"Pay for it, the idea!" said Mrs. College.

"Pay for it with what?" Mr. College wanted to know.

Joe didn't answer. But on the way into the house he pulled a large, horse-choking roll of bills from his pocket, peeled off two twenties and a ten, and tossed them at his father.

"By the way, here's the fifty bucks I owe you," he said.

Mr. College watched goggle-eyed as Joe replaced the roll.

Joe did what is known as ample justice to the unfrugal repast which Mrs. College laid before him, thus confirming her suspicions that he hadn't been eating properly. But Mr. College was in for another rude shock when he asked Joe where he had been staying, and the boy replied casually that he was holing up at The Breakers.

"But the rate there is ten dollars a day!" Mr. College shouted.

"Twenty," yawned Joe, "I have a suite."

Joe's mother insisted that he move back into the cottage with them. Mr. College, who still wasn't convinced that he wouldn't eventually have to pay the hotel bill, didn't object. But Joe, who actually was fed up with hotel life and meals, was careful not to appear too eager.

"I don't know," he said, "I'm mightly comfortable where I am, and I guess maybe I'm a little spoiled with the service and all. You know — bellboys ready to jump every time you snap your fingers, breakfast in bed, private bath — I don't know. How much," he asked, turning to his father, "is the rate here?"

"Why, there's no rate at all, dear," his mother assured him. "The idea! You know this is your home as well as ours, and it always will be."

"Five dollars a day," said Mr. College. "If you can afford to pay twenty at The Breakers you can afford to pay five here. And the first time you snap your fingers at me and holler 'Front, boy,' the rate goes up to twenty."

Joe produced a roll, this time from another pocket, licked his thumb and peeled off two more twenties and a ten, which he tossed at his father.

"Here's a ten-day advance," he said nonchalantly.

Joe arose the next morning a little after nine o'clock, ate a leisurely breakfast, and departed in his Lizzie for the beach. He changed at the bathhouse into his bathing suit, which was composed of blue flannel trunks and a white woolen top with "Life Guard" written across it. Then he set up a beach umbrella on the shore, where he could watch the swimmers, and stretched out on the sand.

Within a matter of minutes, he was surrounded by girls. One of them lit a cigarette and gave it to him. Another insisted on rubbing his face and shoulders with sunburn lotion, although he was already too tan to burn. A third went into the bathhouse, got his ukulele, and tuned it for him. Joe played a few numbers, and the girls sang with him.

But he didn't forget to keep an eye on the swimmers, at the same time. The man who ran the bathhouse knew that Joe was doing his job, and was well satisfied with the way the new life guard was attracting girls to the beach.

Joe was playing host to some twenty girls and a couple of insignificant high-school boys, when his parents walked past in their bathing suits. Since he had decided to keep his father guessing about the source of his income, Joe rolled over on his stomach to hide the "Life Guard" on his jersey. Mr. and Mrs. College waved to him, and he waved back.

Along about noon, after his parents had departed, Joe launched a rowboat to inspect the diving raft and swimmers. The girls fought for the honor of rowing him, and he finally picked two of them — one for each oar. He sat in the stern, giving orders and firmly unfastening the fingers of girls who tried to cling to the gunwales, as the boat slowly circled the raft.

Three other girls, meanwhile, had swum out over their heads and appeared to be drowning. Joe knew they were good enough swimmers, but it was about time for him to take a dip anyway, so he dove over the side of the boat and went through the motions of helping them to shore. Several more girls, who also were good enough swimmers, wanted him to teach them how to swim. He obliged good naturedly, for as long as it suited him. Then, using a speedy Australian crawl, he swam to the raft in a cloud of spray.

He did a swan, a back jackknife, and a gainer and a half — all beautifully executed dives — and seemed to pay no attention to the sighs of admiration from the girls who had followed him to the float. When his two oarsmen brought the rowboat up alongside the raft, he rode in style back to the beach where a dozen or so girls were waiting with towels to dry him off.

By then it was one o'clock and quitting time, so he dressed in the bathhouse, drove his Lizzie by The Breakers to pick up his suitcases, and headed home for lunch.

Mr. and Mrs. College were sitting on the front porch of the cottage when Joe drove up and started to unload the bags.

"Just a minute, dear," Mrs. College called. "Your father will help you with those."

"Front, boy," grunted Mr. College, as he arose from his wicker

The Fellow Who Thought He'd Try His

Dive When No One Was Looking

chair to lend a hand. "Maybe if I disappeared for a couple of weeks I'd get waited on hand and foot around this place, too."

Joe debated whether his father would think it a good joke if he tried to tip him. After noting that Mr. College's chin was outthrust and his lips tightly compressed, Joe decided not to risk it.

For some reason, lunch was not a very congenial meal. Mrs. College seemed worried and Mr. College seemed annoyed. Joe's attempts at small talk didn't go over too well.

"Did you enjoy your swim?" Mr. College asked icily.

"It was the cats," said Joe.

"We saw you taking it easy, surrounded by a horde of girls."

"You're looking at the reason why girls leave home," Joe winked.

"What's on your program this afternoon?"

"The usual, I guess — sailing and tennis." Joe folded his napkin and pushed away from the table. "Got to run. Well, so long. Yours till the kitchen sinks."

"Swimming this morning. Sailing and tennis this afternoon," Mr. College intoned bleakly as Joe drove off in the Model T, with the exhaust whistle howling as usual. "When does he work? Where does he get all that money?"

"Perhaps he has a night job, dear," said Mrs. College, but it was obvious that she was clutching at a straw. "I do hope that all your talk about making money didn't drive the boy into anything dangerous or illegal."

Joe came home to supper that night, and after eating changed into white flannels and a blue-and-white-striped blazer, which was the uniform of Happy Ferdie's Melody Smoothies.

"I'll probably be late — I'm going to the yacht club dance," he informed his parents over his shoulder as he departed. And again the exhaust whistle signaled his departure.

"I guess," said Mrs. College, "this was one of his days off. I must have been wrong about a night job."

"A day off on Thursday? It doesn't seem likely, but maybe so," her husband nodded.

"Perhaps he's been playing the stock market, like everybody else," Mrs. College said brightly. "I'll bet that's it."

"On fifty dollars? I think for the time being you'd better stick to the bet that Thursday is his day off."

But Joe followed the same routine on Friday, Saturday, Sunday, and Monday. Meanwhile, his various rolls of bills, which he flashed upon the slightest provocation and left conspicuously on his dresser at night, were unmistakably growing fatter.

"It's *got* to be the stock market," Mrs. College confided to her husband. "Isn't there something about margin — you know, bears and bulls?"

"I guess you're right," said Mr. College, who knew that the stock market idea was ridiculous. "Why don't you ask him?"

"I don't think we ought to pry into his affairs. Let's just agree that it must be the stock market."

Mr. College nodded, but he believed he had figured out the real source of Joe's income. He didn't want to think about this source, and he didn't want to worry his wife by advancing his theory. In fact the theory was so depressing that he couldn't bring himself to confront Joe with it.

On Monday, Joe made his first legitimate rescue as a life guard. It was high tide, and consequently the distance to the raft was a good deal farther than usual. Nevertheless, a middle-aged

A View of the Boat-Races

couple had undertaken the swim to the raft. Joe was lying on the
beach, surrounded by flappers and playing his ukulele for them.
But he had particularly noticed the middle-aged couple, as they
went into the water, because they were newcomers and still hadn't
picked up a suntan.

He kept an eye on them during their swim to the raft, which
they made easily enough, and then practically forgot about them
while they rested and did a sedate dive or two. But when they
started to swim back into shore, he subconsciously kept an eye on
them again. You had to be particularly careful about newcomers,
who might forget they weren't in as good condition as they used
to be.

The couple was about a third of the way in, when Joe noticed
that the woman seemed to be tiring. He wasn't sure, but to play it
safe he ran to the rowboat and pushed it into the water. When he
looked at the couple again, there was no doubt that the woman
was in trouble. Joe gave the boat another shove, jumped over the
stern, and started rowing. He glanced over his shoulder every few
strokes to be sure his direction was right. And he rowed with every
muscle in his body.

Her husband was trying to help her, and she had both arms
around his neck. They went under once, but came up. And they
went under again just as the boat reached them.

Joe grabbed a life preserver, which was secured to the boat by
a line, and threw it over the side. Then he dove after them.

The woman apparently had let go her grip on her husband,
because Joe came up first with the man. Joe hooked the man's
arms around the life preserver and went down again. He emerged
twice to gulp air, and the third time came up with the woman.

A spontaneous cheer arose from the beach, but Joe scarcely
heard it.

A number of swimmers had arrived to help him, and they got
the couple into the boat. The man was all right, but the woman
was unconscious. Winded but game, Joe rowed the boat slowly

toward shore. Some of the mamas had organized a cheering section, and they shouted, "What's the matter with College? He's all right." Joe heard that cheer plainly, but he was too tired to feel especially elated. Once on the beach again, Joe supervised the application of artificial respiration to the woman. She had been under water only a minute or so, and quickly revived. They wrapped three bathrobes around her, and carried her to her husband's automobile, a fire-engine-red Stutz Bearcat, with an engine not quite so long as a city block and somewhat less low-slung than a snake's hips. Her husband, scarcely taking time to thank Joe, rushed her to a doctor.

Everyone knew that if Joe hadn't been on the job — if he hadn't actually anticipated the trouble — there probably would have been a double drowning. Men in the crowd that had collected clapped him on the back and told him "nice going." Some of the young kids asked if they could feel his muscles, and Joe didn't object. The manager of the bathhouse told him there would be a forty-dollar bonus in his pay envelope on Saturday.

Joe stayed around on the beach until lunchtime, not exactly gloating but certainly well satisfied with himself. By the time he went into the bathhouse to dress, he was completely rested again.

Although he didn't want to admit it to himself, he was also somewhat annoyed that the man he had rescued hadn't been more profuse in his thanks. Of course the man was worried about his wife, but he might at least have shaken Joe's hand.

But the man, sitting in his Stutz, was waiting for Joe in the parking lot, when he came to get his flivver.

"You're the life guard, aren't you?" the man called. "I didn't get a very good look at you before."

"Some car," Joe sighed with ill-concealed envy, as he stopped alongside of it. "How's your wife?"

"She's fine, thanks to you. I took her to the hotel, and the doctor said you had done everything that could be done, and that she'd be feeling as well as ever by tomorrow."

"That's swell," said Joe, who wasn't annoyed any more.

"There's no use my telling you that we're grateful. Besides, I'm a man who believes that actions speak louder than words."

"I just did my job," Joe said modestly, making a circle in the loose dirt with his right sneaker. Then, to change the subject, he added: "That's really a smooth buggy."

"I'm glad you like it."

"How fast will it go?"

"I've had it up to eighty, and there was lots more in it."

"Wow," said Joe.

"I've got the Stutz agency back home. I'm glad you like this one, because it's yours."

"No, it isn't," gulped Joe, hopelessly confused. "That's mine over

A Real Artis

an Artists' Ball

there." He pointed to the disreputable, topless Model T at the side.

"You've just traded that one in on this one," said the man, getting out of the driver's seat and holding the door open for Joe. "I talked it over with my wife, and we want you to have it."

Joe gaped unblinkingly at the Bearcat and at the door which beckoned so invitingly. And then he shook his head.

"I appreciate it," he said. "But I can't take it. I guess it would be like taking a tip, for something that I was supposed to do. And being a Midwestern man . . . Anyway, thanks just the same. Thanks a lot. Tell your wife thanks a lot, too, and I hope she feels better."

Joe retreated hastily to his Model T, set the gas, the spark and the handbrake, and went up front to crank. He hoped the Stutz would disappear before he yielded to temptation. But the man come over and put an arm around Joe's shoulders.

"You really feel that you mustn't accept it?" he asked. "I've got a whole garage full of them, you know. I'd never even miss it."

"Thanks just the same," said Joe. He felt as if he was going to cry, and that would be a fine thing for a Midwestern man who had just rescued two people from drowning.

"Well, listen, son, you'd do me a favor, wouldn't you?"

"I would if it didn't mean changing my mind about not taking the car."

"I've got to go back home tomorrow, and I'm going by train. My wife's staying here, but she doesn't drive. I'll be down weekends for the rest of the summer. While I'm gone, every week, I wish you'd give my car some exercise. It doesn't run right if it stands idle for any length of time. And besides, it's good for business to have a car like this circulating around and being seen at a resort."

"You mean just use it during the week, and you'd take it back at the end of the summer?"

"That's right. As a favor to me. How about it?"

"Wow," hollered Joe.

Some Golf Terms Illustrated and Illuminated—by John Held, Jr.

A birdie.

The mental hazard

Grip, stance and form.

In the rough.

Taking a little turf.

The Petting Green

"Get in it right now. I won't be needing it before I go, so you can drop me off at the hotel. Okay?"

"Home, James," beamed Joe, sliding in behind the wheel, and giving the self-starter a kick.

And so it happened that Joe arrived home for lunch in a fire-engine-red Stutz Bearcat roadster, in which he departed, after eating, for the tennis courts and in which he subsequently departed again for the yacht club dance. His parents carefully refrained at lunch and supper from mentioning the roadster, and Joe himself volunteered no information. But when he finally returned home from the dance, at two o'clock Tuesday morning, still in the Bearcat, his father was waiting up for him.

"Alfred," said Mr. College, "I think it is time for you and me to have a talk."

"Man to man, Pop?" smiled Joe.

"Precisely. And I'm not joking."

"If it's another advance you want on my board, sir," said Joe, producing a roll, which was still growing, and licking his thumb, "why, I can take care . . ."

"Put that damned thing back in your pocket, and don't you even dare flash it or any of those other rolls at me again," Mr. College exploded. "If you must carry all that money around with you, at least get a wallet or something to put it in."

"I've been looking high and low for a money belt," Joe said innocently.

"Where are you getting it, boy?" Mr. College asked dramatically, arms outstretched like Al Jolson. "Where are you getting it?"

"The beans? I'm getting them by working."

"Tell your father the truth, boy," implored Mr. College. "You can confide in your old father."

"I just confided in you, sir. I'm getting the dough by working."

"We've been here now for almost a week," said Mr. College in a resigned whisper. "You've done nothing but go to the beach, play tennis, sail, and dance. Still the money keeps rolling in. And now an expensive red roadster."

"I've gone to picnics, too, sir. Some of my best money comes from picnics. I've got something they all want."

"Whiskey," screamed Mr. College. "That's what I thought. I didn't like to think it about my own flesh and blood, but that's what I thought. You're bootlegging, aren't you?"

"I am not," said Joe indignantly. "What I've got, that they all want, is a picnic service."

"I can't believe it. A College — and a bootlegger! After all the advantages that you've had."

"I am not," repeated Joe.

"Tell me it isn't so, boy. Tell me it isn't so."

"For crying out loud, I've been trying to tell you it isn't, Dad."

"So that's what they've done to my boy at Midwestern. A boot-legger and — yes, I hate to say it — a liar."

"I am not," said Joe.

"If you needed money," declaimed Mr. College, who was so wrapped up in his own performance that he wasn't paying much attention to Joe, "all you had to do was ask me for it."

"I had to get down on my knees to borrow fifty measly beans."

"Have I ever denied you anything? Haven't I always stood behind you, through thick and thin? Haven't I always gone your bail, wired you money, advanced your allowance? Haven't I?"

"Up until this summer, yes. Now listen to me, will you, Dad?"

"I'm listening," said Mr. College in martyred tones.

"The Stutz isn't mine."

"I see," said Mr. College, who obviously didn't believe a word of it. "Whose is it, then?"

"Well, doggone," laughed Joe, snapping his fingers. "I forgot to ask him his name. But honest, Pop, he's a man I met today at the beach."

"A man you met today at the beach," Mr. College parroted. "And he walked up to you, I suppose, introduced himself, without

The Laughing Stock

mentioning his name, and asked you if you'd like to borrow his car."

"It wasn't like that at all," Joe protested. "You're putting words in my mouth. You see, I had just finished saving him and his wife from drowning. Naturally, he was grateful, and . . ."

"Oh, oh, oh," yelped Mr. College, beating his temples and rocking forward and backward in grief. "To think that my own son would make up such a barefaced lie and throw it in my very teeth."

It took quite a while for Joe to explain the entire situation and an even longer time for him to convince his father that the explanation was the truth. But when Mr. College finally was convinced, he was beaming from ear to ear.

Now it was Mr. College who reached into his pocket. He produced a thick wallet and extracted two fifties.

"You're a chip off the old block, Alfred," he crowed, flipping the money to his son. "Wrap these around the outside of one of your beanbags."

"You're convinced now I'm not bootlegging, Pop?" Joe rubbed it in.

"Convinced!" Mr. College scoffed. "We Colleges are all close-mouthed about business transactions, Alfred. I knew that the only way I could make you talk was to confront you with something ridiculous, like that."

"Well, I'll be darned," said Joe.

"How much have you saved up so far?"

"I guess I'd better be close-mouthed about that, Pop," grinned Joe. "There's more business than I can handle, and I wish I could talk you into going partners with me."

"Don't get too big for your Plus Fours," Mr. College warned.

"Okay. But I'll tell you one thing — you're wasting your time at the agency."

CHAPTER 9

"How do we know," Alfred College asked his wife, "what sort of girls Richard will take up with when he goes to Midwestern? The girls he knows around here are bad enough. But at least we've had a chance to meet them and to try to steer him away from the worst of them."

"There's nothing wrong with his girls," said Betty College.

"Suppose some girl at Midwestern, who thinks he has money or something, decides she's going to hook him. See what I mean? You know yourself that nine-tenths of the girls at co-educational colleges are there just because they're looking for husbands."

"Well, I like that!" said Mrs. College.

If Joe had economized that summer, he might have saved a really substantial sum of money. But even with the gracious living to which he treated himself, he had managed to save seven hundred dollars by the time the fall term opened at Midwestern.

His father advised Joe repeatedly to bank the money, for a rainy day. But Joe replied that, now he had learned how easy it was to accumulate beans, he felt safe in saying that it ain't gonna rain no more. Joe even suggested that, if his father wanted to ride a *real* gravy train, he should prepare to let Joe manage the family's finances.

This was especially annoying to Mr. College, since Joe's mother also seemed to think there was a great deal of merit in the boy's suggestion. Mrs. College kept repeating that, after all, the proof of the pudding was in the eating, wasn't it?

Joe used his savings to buy a completely new set of traps, includ-

emy of Bass Drum Decorators

ing a bass drum with lights that flashed like Rudy Toody's. Mr.
College said that the purchase showed just how little the boy knew
about the value of money. And since Joe was broke again, his
father had to pay the charges to express the traps to Midwestern.

Back at school that autumn, Joe slipped easily into the routine
of fraternity life. It was good to see Betty again, too. They went
canoeing on their first date, and Joe wasn't really too displeased to
discover that she still believed nice girls only necked vertically.

Although Joe's allowance should have been ample, he found it could no longer support him in the manner to which he had become accustomed. Consequently, after a week of classes, he decided to turn his money-making talents to good advantage.

Tennis and sailing lessons were out of the question. But Joe thought that, with the experience he had gained from the Melody Smoothies, he should be able to organize his own band.

Joe had firmly intended to select his musicians on the basis of talent. But many of his fraternity brothers wanted to supplement their allowances, too, and Joe couldn't very well turn them down. Also, Betty wanted to be the vocalist, and Joe didn't see how he could turn her down, either.

Still, he was confident that the ability of his musicians would improve. He was so sure that he knew how to make money, and he had become so accustomed to spending it, that he soon was in debt almost six hundred dollars. He had bought tailor-made blazers and flannels for all of the band. He had bought Betty a sequin-studded, flesh-colored evening dress. He had bought blanket-sized pennants, with "Joe College" written on them, to hang as a backdrop. And he had bought megaphones, embossed with "J. C.," for himself, Betty, and all the other members of the group.

He charged some of the articles and purchased the others on the installment plan.

There was no demand whatsoever for the services of the band. What Joe apparently had failed to take into account was that, while there was a scarcity of college boys at the shore, there was an abundance of them at Midwestern. And a good many of them had their own bands.

The first two engagements, which Joe managed to land by cutting his price almost to nothing, turned out miserably. Betty couldn't sing and the musicians couldn't play very well separately and couldn't play at all as a unit. Everyone connected with the band realized almost immediately how terrible they were, and wanted to quit. That would have suited Joe, except that his creditors were beginning to hang around the fraternity house and follow him to classes. By pleas and threats, Joe managed to hold the band together until its third performance.

This performance was at an alumni dance, given by a neighboring fraternity on the Friday night before the first home football game of the season. Joe had received an advance payment of thirty dollar to play at the dance, and he intended to see that his band lived up to its commitment.

By then, Joe College's Collegians were thoroughly demoralized. The first two engagements, in dining rooms of local hotels, had resulted in an emptying of tables within a matter of minutes. The irate managers, stuck with kitchens full of cooked food, had threatened to sue, and Joe had led his artists out of the hotels via the servants' entrances.

Most of the Collegians, still reluctantly willing to help Joe but ashamed of the reception which they knew would await them, started drinking long before the third performance. Also, they refused to show up ahead of time to help drape the pennants and prepare the bandstand. Those chores, consequently, fell to Joe and Betty, who then awaited nervously the arrival of their colleagues.

When the rest of the band appeared, Joe knew he was in for real trouble. The members were unanimously plastered. Doc, who played the banjo, was especially so.

The Collegians, hilarious now rather than ashamed, took their places on the bandstand. There was frightening bedlam for a few minutes, while they tuned their instruments or tried to. Then Joe, determined to make a brave show of it, picked up his baton, smiled artificially, and hit two sharp licks with the baton on the edge of the piano. The Collegians started to play.

Booze may have helped many a jazz band, but it was no help at all to the Collegians, who weren't sure what number they were supposed to be playing and certainly didn't care. Joe tried to stop them, but for the first time they were having fun on a bandstand, and they all went their separate unmusical ways. It was murder.

Joe, who was sober and wished he weren't, finally got silence.

THE PROPER STUDY OF MANKIND
IS MAN BUT— *It's awfully hard to stick to it*

According to John Held, Jr.

The freshman year.

The sophomore year.

The junior year.

The senior year.

Betty, also sober, started to tiptoe away, and Joe didn't have the heart to stop her. In fact he breathed a sigh of relief when he saw she was out of danger.

"Let's try it again, fellows," Joe begged, his face crimson. "It's 'Five Foot Two,' remember? Ready now?"

"All set, maestro," Doc assured him.

Ill-concealed threats mingled with pleas for mercy from the dance floor, and the dance chairman pushed his way forward.

"That's all for you guys," said the chairman. "Give me back my thirty bucks and beat it. We'll use the phonograph."

"I haven't got your thirty bucks," said Joe, who had given all the money he had to his most insistent creditor.

"We came here to play," Doc said, pushing the chairman, "and we're going to play. What did you stop us for, Joe? We were going swell."

The chairman pushed back. Doc wound up like a tennis player getting ready to serve, and swung his banjo. The face of the banjo was made of some kind of hide, and it popped loudly as the frame settled dog-collar fashion around the neck of the chairman. Someone slugged Doc and he sat down hard on Joe's new bass drum, whose lights continued to flash on and off, even though the drum itself was inhabited.

In the ensuing melee, megaphones were trampled and pennants and custom-made clothes hopelessly torn and bloodied. By the time the police arrived to escort the Collegians to the cooler, the assets of the band amounted to exactly zero.

Word of the arrests spread quickly through the town. Joe's creditors got to the police station almost as soon as the Black Maria containing the still hilarious and loudly singing Collegians, and their worried director.

"Who's the leader of this band?" demanded the desk sergeant.

Joe, who was standing as far away from the sergeant's desk as the law would allow, was pushed forward by his musicians.

"He is," they pronounced in chorus. Joe thought bitterly that it

"I think that colts are just too comical—they seem to be all legs."

was the first time they had been in unison since the orchestra was formed.

"I am," Joe agreed unenthusiastically.

"Well, come up here where I can see you."

The Collegians gave Joe another push, and he braked to a halt a few inches from the sergeant's face.

"What's your name — as if I didn't know," said the sergeant. "You again, Joe College?"

"This time, your honor," Joe assured him, "it's not my fault."

"It ain't never your fault," the sergeant nodded. "It ain't your fault when you hoist bloomers over City Hall, and it ain't your

When fashion gets flip with a flapper!

fault when you're caught pouring bootleg hooch into a flapper at
The Green Parrot. Your band started a fight, didn't it?"

"I guess so."

"Ain't you the leader of the band?"

"All right, your honor. It's my fault."

"Who are these other people?" the sergeant asked, indicating
the creditors.

"In a manner of speaking," mumbled Joe, "they're our sponsors."

"You owe them money, eh?"

"A little."

"How much altogether?"

"Six hundred beans, I guess."

The sergeant pointed to a telephone. "Call him," he ordered.

"Call who, your honor?"

"Who do you always call? Your old man, of course. Call him collect, too, remember."

"How much is bail?"

"This time only costs — fifteen dollars, if you pay your debts." The sergeant raised his voice so that the creditors would be sure to hear him. "I ain't going to have you kids from out of town try to cheat our outstanding citizens and voters."

There was a slight delay while the long-distance call went through, and Joe tried to think of a tactful way to approach his father. He guessed there wasn't any tactful way. Then his father was on the phone, and Joe hastily outlined the situation.

For some reason, Mr. College seemed to think it was extremely amusing.

"Haw, haw, haw," he roared, so loudly that Joe had to hold the receiver away from his ear. "So you went into business for yourself, and this time you lost your shirt and they arrested you. Haw, haw, haw."

"Yes, sir," said Joe. "Will you wire the money?"

"So you ought to handle the family finances," Mr. College guffawed. "And you need six hundred dollars to pay off your creditors and fifteen dollars to pay off the police. Why don't you use your beanbag?"

"You know I spent that, Dad," Joe pleaded. "Will you wire it?"

"I will on one condition," said Mr. College. "That set of traps you bought cost seven hundred dollars, didn't it? Well, you sell those traps and send me whatever you get for them. Fair enough?"

"Fair enough," Joe agreed. "More than fair."

"So you'll learn the value of money after all," crowed Mr. College. "Fair enough?"

"Fair enough," Joe repeated. "Thanks a lot, Pop. I'll be waiting for the wire."

Entrance Examination

"EXPLAIN THIS BLACK BOTTOM DANCE."
"YOU DON'T LET YOUR RIGHT HIP KNOW WHAT YOUR LEFT HIP IS DOING."

Joe hung up. He figured he might get a dollar or two for the mashed traps, perhaps as kindling wood. But he saw no particular reason why he should have mentioned that over the phone. That was the sort of subject, Joe thought, that might better be handled in a letter.

An army of alumni, including most of last year's seniors, had returned to Joe's fraternity house for the Ohio State game, which opened the home football season. Joe and Betty sat on a hammock on the front porch early Saturday afternoon, with their feet propped up on the porch rail. A new group of pledges was raking leaves from the front lawn. Streams of cars and pedestrians were filing past the house toward the stadium.

Many of the fraternity's alumni were already feeling pretty good. You could hear them singing and laughing loudly inside the house. Most stewed of all were last year's seniors, pretending now to be careworn businessmen; pretending to find campus life and the undergraduate brothers juvenile to the extreme. Perhaps last year's seniors were drinking heavily because they realized for the first time that college — yes, and youth itself — was gone forever and could never be recaptured.

College boys hawking programs — "Names, numbers, ages, and salaries of all the players in your official program, here" — and old men hawking chrysanthemums, pennants and toy-football badges, were in the crowd moving toward the stadium.

From the distance there were drumbeats, and motorcycle policemen cleared the street for the Midwestern Band, marching to the game. As the beats grew louder, the brothers and alumni emerged from the house and crowded onto the porch and lawn.

The band struck up the Midwestern Victory Song. A roar went up from the throng, and Joe could feel goose pimples rising on his forearms.

The band came into sight, then, one hundred and twenty strong

The U:

tletoe

Ursula: IS MY NOSE SHINY, DEARIE?
Lambert: NO, BUT YOUR RIGHT KNEE IS DUSTY.

— cocky, grinning, blowing, beating — wearing tassled shakos and uniforms of Midwestern orange and black. A six foot eight drum major, who was center on the basketball team during the winter months, strutted at the front of the column.

The crowd started to sing with the music — "Our big team will do or die, boys, or known the reason why, boys."

Billy, the old ram mascot, brought up the rear wearing a Midwestern football blanket and being led by four cartwheel-turning cheerleaders.

The noisy, back-slapping crowd flowed into the street again. The music grew fainter. Finally only the beat of drums, fading in the distance, could be heard.

Most of the pedestrians had Midwestern pennants, but a few Buckeye supporters, with Ohio State pennants, were in evidence. Occasionally a Midwestern man would reach forward and jerk

"It's all right, Santa—you can come in. My parents still believe in you."

the porkpie of an Ohio State rooter down around his ears, so that
the hat looked like an over-sized derby. But the Ohio visitors took
it all good-naturedly.

Automobiles, many flying twisted streamers of crepe paper, tried
in vain to nudge through the mob of pedestrians. The pedestrians
wouldn't give way, so the cars couldn't move faster than a walk.
Ten or twelve student pedestrians were hitching rides on the
bumpers, fenders, and radiators of every car.

"Gee, it's really the cats, isn't it?" sighed Betty, sliding over in
the hammock so that she touched Joe. "I don't know; it does something to me — like marching off to war, I guess, except without the
tears."

The brothers and the alumni had left the porch and joined the
throng heading for the stadium. Joe slipped a hand under a pillow,
and so did Betty. It happened to be the same pillow.

Joe looked behind him, to make certain the porch was empty.

"Not *here*," Betty said. But Joe kissed her just the same, and for
a coed who only necked vertically it was an entirely satisfactory
kiss.

"You ought to be ashamed — in broad daylight, and with all
those people out there in the street," Betty protested, in a voice
without the slightest conviction. She squeezed his hand.

"Does your mother know you're out?" Joe teased.

"Not with you, Daddy, thank goodness!"

"Do you still want to — after we graduate, I mean?" Joe whispered.

"Do I want to *what?*"

"You know, what we talked about at the house party."

"We talked about a lot of things."

"You know what I mean."

"I wouldn't be wearing this," Betty smiled, nodding toward the
fraternity pin fastened to her dress, "if I'd changed my mind."

"Gee," said Joe.

"Ain't we," sighed Betty, "got fun?"

From the stadium, a quarter of a mile away, rumbled the thunder of a cheer.

"Guess we'd better shove along, if we're going to get there in time to watch the big team warm up," Joe said at last.

"I guess so."

"You got the pennants?"

"Right here," answered Betty, picking them up from the porch rail. "You got what you're supposed to bring?"

"Right here," replied Joe, thumping something in his breast pocket which echoed gurglingly. "Straws?"

"Right here." Betty produced two from her handbag. "A girl can't be too careful of her rep, you know."

Joe sighed happily, and so did Betty. They were reluctant to leave the hammock, but of course they wouldn't have missed the activities in the stadium for a month's allowance.

"Let's shake that thing, then," said Joe, getting up and helping Betty.

They shook that thing, down the steps, down the sidewalk, and into the crowd in the street. The street was lined with maples, covered with scarlet leaves, and the sun set fire to them.

Joe pushed his porkpie jauntily to the back of his head. He wished that every day, forever after, could be a football Saturday, with Betty, at Midwestern.

CHAPTER 10

SINCE ALFRED was too nervous to get behind the wheel, Betty College drove the family to the station the night young Richard was to depart for Midwestern. They said goodbye on the platform. Richard kissed his mother and shook hands with his father.

"Now don't forget what I've told you," Alfred cautioned his son for the fifth time.

"Don't panic, Pop," Richard grinned. "I can take care of myself. Everything's going to be real George all the way."

"Real what?"

"Hunky-dory, peaches and cream, jake," translated Betty.

"Remember, you're going to college to get an education," Alfred continued, "not to have a four-year picnic. It's a serious business, and . . ."

"No tiger sweat, no, chicks," recited Richard. "We've been through it over and over. Please don't get your dandruff up again, Pop."

"No hooch, no mamas and don't get in a stew," Betty translated again.

"All I ask, boy," Alfred said dramatically, "is that you try to remember one thing. If you're confronted with temptation; if anyone tries to lead you astray — just remember that your mother and I want to be proud of you. And if you remember that, well . . ."

"In other words," Betty told her son, glancing innocently at Alfred, "don't do anything your father wouldn't have done. Isn't that what you're trying to say, dear?"

"HASN'T SCRATCHED YET!"

THE
SWEET
GIRL
GRADUATE

Alfred looked at her incredulously, and started to deny it. Then, with the dignity of a Substantial Citizen, he pulled himself together. He wrinkled his forehead sternly, stroked his bald spot, and cleared his throat impressively.

"Precisely," he said.